DANCER DRAGON

BODYGUARD SHIFTERS #6

ZOE CHANT

Dancer Dragon

Author's Note

All books in this series contain a standalone romance with an HEA, but this one is slightly less standalone than most. Previous books in this series (particularly *Pet Rescue Panther* and *Day Care Dragon*) provide more backstory on these characters. This book can be read and enjoyed without having read the other books, but you'll learn more about the main characters in those books.

Here is the complete series in order:
1. **Bearista** (Derek & Gaby's book)
2. **Pet Rescue Panther** (Ben & Tessa's book)
3. **Bear in a Bookshop** (Gunnar & Melody's book)
4. **Day Care Dragon** (Darius & Loretta's book)
5. **Bull in a Tea Shop** (Maddox & Verity's book)
6. **Dancer Dragon** (Heikon & Esme's book)
7. **Babysitter Bear** (Dan & Paula's book)

And don't miss the spinoff series, Stone Shifters:
1. **Stoneskin Dragon** (Reive & Jess's book)
2. **Stonewing Guardian** (Mace & Thea's book)

You may also enjoy Bodyguard Shifters Collection 1, collecting books 1-4.

PROLOGUE: TWENTY YEARS AGO

The moon was bright, and Esmerelda Lavigna couldn't sleep.

She pushed back the sumptuous, gold-chased bedspread and winced a little as her bare feet touched the cold stone floor, until she groped around with her toes and found the soft, embroidered slippers by the bed. A heavy sweater lay across the back of the chair beside the bed. She pulled it over her silk nightgown.

The room's tall windows painted the room in silver moonlight. Esme padded over to look out. Below her, the mountain fell away in stepped terraces of gardens and farms and pastures, some of them glittering with fairy lights, others dark beneath the moon. Here and there, a small glow dotted the hillside where someone in the extended Corcoran clan might still be awake.

She unlatched the window and opened it. A cool breeze blew into her room, filled with the bracing scents of the night and the perfume of night-blooming flowers. Inside her chest, Esme's dragon uncoiled and spread its wings. *Are we going to fly?* it asked.

Esme leaned out and smiled when she discovered that the windows were tall and wide enough that she could easily step out, with nothing beneath her but a sheer drop down the mountainside. This place was called the Aerie, and it had been built by and for dragons, with their needs in mind.

But right now, she didn't want to fly as much as she wanted to find someone specific.

Later, dear, she promised her dragon, and latched the window.

She crossed the floor and stepped out into the hall. It was long and dim, lit only by similarly tall windows at the far end. Esme paused at the door next to hers and listened quietly, then tested the knob. Finding it unlocked, she opened it carefully and peeked inside.

In a big four-post bed like the one she'd just gotten out of, a tangle of dark hair was visible on a white pillow. Esme's teenage daughter Melody was deeply asleep, one fist tucked up under her cheek like a much younger child.

Esme smiled to herself. Her little girl would be safe here, protected within a fortress that no enemy could penetrate, while Esme herself wandered the mountain. She closed the door with a soft click and went down the hall, her steps quickening until the long white skirt of her nightgown swirled out behind her. By the time she reached the stairs at the end of the hall, she was humming to herself in a rapture of delight. Music filled her heart and soul, a wordless song of love. She couldn't *wait* to see him again.

Who would have believed that being with any man could feel like this? She was a mature dragon, hundreds of years old. She had taken other lovers throughout her long life. But *this* romance made her feel like a teenager in the first flush of young love.

That was the magic of the mate bond.

Eagerness gave wings to her slippered feet as she all but

flew up the stairs. She didn't even have to wonder where *he* was. All she had to do was follow her dragon's silent yearning.

And she found him a few levels above the guest suites, standing on a balcony, silhouetted in the moonlight.

"Heikon," Esme called softly.

He turned, the moonlight casting his handsome face and high brow in stark relief. He seemed pensive, even troubled, but the expression evaporated as soon as he saw her. "My love," he murmured, and hearing those words in his deep voice lifted Esme's soul. Her feet, it seemed, barely touched the floor as she crossed the room, and Heikon Corcoran took her hands in his, and then took her in his arms.

"You're chilly," he murmured, stroking her tumbling mass of unbound hair.

"I couldn't wait until tomorrow to see you." It was foolish. *She* was foolish. She was no girl, to be swept off her feet; she was a grown woman with a teenage daughter sleeping downstairs.

But Heikon only laughed. "Fly with me?"

"I thought you'd never ask."

They stepped off the balcony together and shifted in midair. His dragon was gunmetal blue, gleaming cobalt and silver in the moonlight; hers was deep emerald green, with her scales patterned in gold like the glint of sunlight through leaves.

Around and around, they flew together in the nighttime sky, their great winged bodies twining together. It was a dragon's mating dance, and when finally they touched down in the gardens, they were both breathless as they shifted back.

Heikon caught her in mid-step with a gentle hand on her elbow, and stood looking down at her, eyes dark with desire. Above him the fairy lights twinkled. Like tiny captive stars, strings of white-gold lights were twined in every trellis and tree, turning the garden to a wonderland beneath the moon.

She had never seen anything more beautiful than Heikon's garden ... except Heikon himself. She still couldn't believe it had only been a week since she'd accepted an invitation from Heikon to visit the Aerie. The invitation was aimed mainly at her daughter (he was seeking mates for his clan scions, she knew)—and as soon as her eyes had met his, she'd known, they'd both known. And they'd laughed about it, because in all their long lives, through all the dealings between the Lavigna and Corcoran clans, they had never met face to face before.

"Turn around," Heikon said to her now, and she did. Around them, the fairy lights glimmered under the moon. The wind changed direction, and a wave rolled across her of the same rich perfume smell she'd noticed from her window, along with a shower of tumbling petals.

She reached up and laughed, brushing petals out of her hair. "What are these? They smell wonderful."

"Cherry blossoms. Sakura trees, imported from Japan. You and your daughter are just in time for them. Another couple of weeks and you'd have missed them completely."

"I didn't know cherry trees grew this far north, or this high in the mountains." She and Melody had flown over snow on their way here.

"This valley is sheltered, and warmer than the surrounding hills."

She hadn't even noticed that they weren't in the same gardens she had explored by daylight. This was a different part of Heikon's mountain, with walls of stone towering above them, enclosing them in a small south-facing canyon.

"My cherry trees grow all over this mountain," Heikon said. "There are some blooming in other parts of the garden. But this is my garden's sheltered heart."

He said it with hushed reverence. Esme wondered if he could possibly mean ... but no, she thought; she was reading too much into a simple sentence. Someone as old and guarded as Heikon could not possibly move that fast, even with the mate bond supporting and nurturing their relationship. Anyway, she had heard rumors about the Heart of Heikon's hoard, and it wasn't a grove of trees. Heikon's clan were one of the ones who employed human Heart-keepers. Esme had always found it a rather strange custom, but she was determined not to judge, considering what her own hoard's Heart was.

Unfortunately, her brain was determined not to cooperate. Trying not to think about the many differences between their clans only made her think of all the other things she was trying not to think about.

"What is it?" Heikon asked, brushing her lip with his thumb. "You were radiant a moment ago. Do cherry trees make you sad?"

"No, it's not the trees. I was only thinking of all the time we've lost. I wish that I had met you long ago, before so much else came between us. Before Darius ..." She spoke the name of her former lover with some embarrassment. Things had been over with Darius for years, but she wished now that she hadn't given him those years of her life, years that she could have spent with Heikon, had she but known.

"Shhh," Heikon whispered, and his lips touched her cheek, her neck. "There will always be a past for those who live as long as we do. I have long-grown children myself, with children of their own. But no other lover can compare ..." He brushed a red ringlet away from her cheek. "... to the one whose soul fits yours like the other half of a puzzle piece."

"The one voice that is perfect harmony for yours," she said, and playfully tweaked his jacket. "If I could only get you to sing with me. Or dance."

"I was dancing with you only a moment ago."

"I mean on land."

He smiled fondly down at her. "Give me time. You can't teach an old dragon new tricks in one night. We have a whole long lifetime to teach each other new things."

True, she thought, and her heart fluttered all over again. "In the morning, perhaps," she offered, stroking her hand across his lightly stubbled cheek.

He caught her hand, pressed it against his skin. "Ah, love. In the morning I hope you'll accept my offer of an escort back to your home in the city."

"What?" she said, pulling her hand away in surprise. "What happened to 'all the time in the world'? What happened to 'I can't get enough of you, Esmerelda'?"

His smile was wistful. "It's true. We *do* have all the time in the world, and I can't get enough of your skin and never will. But for now, just for now, I think you and your daughter would best be elsewhere. I will come join you as soon as I can."

"What are you talking about?" She looked up at him, searching his moon-shadowed face and his dark eyes, and seeing, now, the pensive concern she'd noticed earlier. "Is something happening? What's wrong?"

"Only a little internal trouble within the clan. It's nothing to worry about, but I'd feel better about it if you'd take your daughter elsewhere for a time. You were talking earlier about how much you wanted to visit Greece before the weather turns hot. This might be a nice time of year for it."

"What—you want me to leave the *country*? What is this trouble, Heikon?"

"Nothing much, I hope. I just want to be sure you're well out of it, while I take care of it. Then I can come join you and your daughter in Greece." He stroked a hand down the side of her face. "I'd love to see you in a bikini on the beach. Not that you aren't lovely in any attire."

"This is ridiculous. I can't believe we've both found our mates after *centuries*, and now you want me to leave."

"For a few days," he promised. "A week at most. Then we can begin our life together properly. But I need to do a few things first, so we can do it in peace and safety."

"A week," she sighed. Well, she'd waited a lifetime for him; what was one week more? She could go visit the Heart of her hoard in the Greek sea caves, and lounge around on the beach with her daughter. And when Heikon arrived, she could take him there, to the most private and personal thing any dragon possessed.

It occurred to her that she very much wanted to take him there.

She started to open her mouth to tell him, but then closed it again. She would make it a surprise, a lovely surprise.

"One week," she said. "You promise?"

"I promise." He bent to kiss her, and between kisses he murmured, "One week. And then we will never be apart again."

She could feel the truth of the promise thrumming along the bond between them. With that in mind, all her earlier ardor from the mating flight came back, and she reached for his jacket, pulling it down to expose broad shoulders. He slid the sweater from her shoulders, and cupped her breast through her nightgown. She threw back her head so he could mouth at her exposed throat, and he put his arms around her and laid her down beneath the cherry trees.

A week, she thought, with a small part of her brain as the rest of her was given over to delight.

A week wasn't so very long. She could wait a week. As for the risk that it might take more than a week ... well, he was her mate and he wouldn't lie to her. All the betrayals of a long lifetime had taught her not to trust, but now she was determined to start over anew. She would trust him in everything. She would open up her heart as if it was fresh and new to love, and had never been burned. That was what being mates meant. Her mate would never betray her.

He had promised. After one short week, they would never be apart again.

ESME

TWENTY YEARS LATER

When she had last set foot in the Aerie, Esme had been twenty years younger, a woman in the first flush of a new love. She had spun across these stone floors in the steps to her own personal dance, with her heart buoyed by a music only she could hear.

Now she was older, wiser, and a great deal more cynical, and there was no mate bond anymore.

It still seemed that she could feel it, like the ache of a phantom limb. Once, the severed bond had been the source of an agony and a grief so severe that she thought she would die from it. If not for Melody, she might have. But she couldn't abandon her daughter, and so, one slow step at a time, she had dragged herself back from that terrible, ragged edge.

And now she was back here, in a place she'd sworn she would never again set foot, and the cold place where the mate bond had once been was aching anew, like a scar that never really healed.

Could not heal.

But the Aerie, too, had its scars. Esme walked through the

halls she vaguely remembered, and found them shockingly changed, and not just from the recent battle as Heikon's clan clashed with the ancestral enemies of the dragons, the gargoyles. The threads of this damage ran much deeper. The hallway had been remodeled; the once-huge windows were smaller now, impossible to climb out of and go flying under the moon.

"Lady Esmerelda!" The voice was somehow familiar, but she didn't recognize it until an Asian woman in black leather armor hurried to her and clasped her hands. "Thank you for coming to help us in our time of need."

"Hello, Anjelica." She couldn't remember exactly how the woman fit into Heikon's large and complicated family tree, but they had met briefly when she was here before, twenty years ago. Did Anjelica know that she had been Heikon's mate at the time? This raised an entire new specter of awkwardness. Most people in both their clans had not known they were mates. They had kept it private—not the romance itself, because there was no way to hide that, but the fact that it was not just a romantic tryst, but a mate-bonding. The implications were too huge, with Heikon being the Corcoran clanlord and Esme closely related to the entire Lavigna power structure. It was going to be a very big deal, a formal alliance between the Corcoran and Lavigna clans, and neither of them wanted to deal with the social and political ramifications until they'd had some time just for each other first.

It had all made perfect sense at the time. She had been in love, and determined to start her new life with Heikon as if she had no past, as fresh and innocent as if she had never been hurt before. Keeping their bond to themselves had made sense to her at the time. Now it looked like the naivety of a child, especially since she didn't know how many of Heikon's clan would look at her and see all that she had lost.

"I'm afraid many of our guest suites have been damaged," Anjelica said, turning to escort Esme along the hallway. She looked somewhat damaged herself; there was a large bandage on her cheek, and one of her arms was in a sling. "But we'll find a place for you. Lord Heikon has instructed that you are to have nothing but the best."

"I'm sure." Esme was too annoyed to keep the frost out of her voice. "Too busy to greet me in person, is he?"

Anjelica looked away. "He's very busy, with everything that's happened ..."

She knows. Esme couldn't say exactly how she knew, but something in Anjelica's guilty posture let her know that Anjelica not only remembered her from all those years ago, but also remembered what she had been then. What she was no longer.

How did you explain it to them, Heikon? she thought, in sudden cold fury. *How did you convince your closest advisors to accept you showing up with a mate, and then one day having none?*

She knew, secondhand, that Heikon's clan had been through a great many upheavals since she'd last been to the Aerie. There had been an attempted coup, a great many deaths, and now the war with the gargoyles. They'd certainly had their problems.

But none of that excused the greatest betrayal that one shifter could visit upon another.

How do you convince your clan to follow you, Heikon, knowing that you willingly broke your mate bond?

Only his inner circle knew it, she was sure. Anjelica and perhaps a few others. Heikon had never properly trusted people; he wouldn't have told them. As she had learned all too well, he didn't even trust his own mate.

The thought occurred to her that she could tell them. She could destroy him with a word.

Perhaps she would.

"Here is your suite, Lady Esme," Anjelica said, still without meeting her eyes. The door was wedged in its frame, and Anjelica had to throw her weight against it to get it to open. The entire mountain was like that: corridors slightly askew, window glass cracked, doors out of kilter. When Esme stepped into her room, she found that it was covered with dust that had sifted down from the ceiling during the battle. The copper ewer full of water was overturned on the floor, soaking the once-colorful rugs and turning their load of dust into a soupy, muddy mess.

"I'm sorry for the state of the room." Embarrassment was now written all over Anjelica's face. "I'll send someone to clean it up. I'm sorry, I can't stay; I have to go see to the wounded."

And with that, some of Esme's anger evaporated. She was not so petty as to complain about substandard accommodations when the entire mountain had nearly been destroyed, its people hurt and killed. "It's all right," she said. It wasn't, but she would have it out with Heikon later. Heikon, who still hadn't shown up, who couldn't even look her in the eyes. "Can I help? I don't know much about nursing, but I could fetch and carry things, or perhaps look after the children. I have a child of my own, you know."

"If you could," Anjelica said with tremendous relief, "we would very much appreciate it."

Turning her back on the ruined suite was something of a relief for Esme as well. This wasn't the same room where she'd stayed twenty years ago—the mountain was so different now that she wasn't even certain if she could find it —but it was similar enough to strike a painful chord of memory. That wasn't the bed where she'd dreamed sweet fantasies about Heikon, but it might as well have been.

I was a fool to come here, she thought as she followed

Anjelica back down the stairs to the makeshift infirmary on the lower levels of the mountain. *I should have stayed away.*

She was here, mainly, out of friendship for her old ex-lover, Darius. Although things had been over between them decades ago, she hadn't been willing to let him face the gargoyles alone. Helping save Heikon's clan was an incidental side effect. If it were up to Esme, she'd have let them fall.

Or at least she thought so, until she saw the infirmary with all its wounded. Some of them were still in dragon form, too hurt to shift back. Esme sighed and picked up a roll of bandages.

No. She couldn't have let them all die. *They* didn't deserve it, no matter what their clanlord had done all those years ago.

She hoped she wouldn't encounter Darius among the wounded. She knew he'd been wounded in the battle. But there was no sign of him, so presumably he was off being tended by his human mate, Loretta.

Esme wished them well, with an earnest unselfishness that genuinely surprised her. It was nice to see Darius happy, and Loretta was good for him.

Still, that didn't mean she wanted to *see* him, or the two of them, being mated and happy and all the things Esme no longer could say about herself.

The mate bond no longer connected her to Heikon, so she no longer had any sense of him: no idea if he was in the mountain or elsewhere, nor if he was hurt or well. But nevertheless, whether by chance or by some lingering vestige of it, she happened to be looking up when he walked into the room.

He looked no older—but then, he wouldn't. Twenty years was nothing to a dragon who was already more than four hundred when she'd met him. Bronze skin, dark hair laced thoroughly with iron-gray, a high forehead and sharp cheekbones. It was an aristocratic face, a face she'd once found beautiful.

She still found it beautiful. She still wanted to soften when she looked at him.

He had given her up, she reminded herself. He had given *them* up. In twenty years, he'd never once attempted to contact her. Never let her know that the sudden severing of the mate bond had not meant his death, but rather, an intentional disconnection on his end. She'd had to find out that he was alive secondhand, from *Darius* of all people, two years ago.

She hadn't even known it was possible to sever a mate bond, until realizing that Heikon had somehow done it. Since learning he was still alive, she'd looked into it, trying to understand what had happened, and had learned that certain poisons were rumored to do away with the mate bond. Heikon must have taken one of those. Essence of dragonsbane was the most likely one.

The man she had known twenty years ago was a firm but fair leader, not a cruel man. With the danger in the clan, he must have set her free in the mistaken belief that he was protecting her.

But what it came down to was that he had poisoned himself rather than remain mated to her. Never once had he asked what *she* wanted. Never once had he given her the option of choosing to stay and face the danger with him. No, he had sent her away like a ... like a *child*, and then he had cut the bond.

She reminded herself firmly of that. No matter how much she wanted to like him, no matter how much she missed what they'd had, and no matter how sympathetic his reasons, he had taken it away, and he'd done it on purpose. All that they once had was gone, because of him.

He was talking to Anjelica by the door. Maybe he would

leave without seeing her. She rolled a bandage with brisk, aggressive twists of her hands. She hoped he'd leave. She hoped he'd stay. She hoped he'd give her a chance to yell at him properly.

In some small, weak corner of her soul, she hoped the mate bond would roar back to life the moment he turned and his eyes met hers.

And then he did turn.

His face went still and startled. His eyes were just the same as she remembered, dark and piercing and utterly arresting.

Deep inside, her dragon stirred, rising with a sudden surge of hope.

But there was no miraculous reawakening of the mate bond. Where once she had seen his dragon in his eyes, now she saw only the man.

Her dragon sank back in disappointment, and she turned away: furious with him, and furious with herself for hoping.

HEIKON

For twenty years, Esme Lavigna had filled Heikon's thoughts during the day, and his dreams at night.

He was still unprepared for the effect on him of actually seeing her.

She must have come to the infirmary straight from the battle with the gargoyles, because she was dusty and smudged, rather than her usual put-together self. Her thick red-gold hair was coming out of its braid. There was a bruise on one cheek, and she looked tired.

She looked like a warrior goddess just back from a fight.

She also looked incandescently furious with him. While he stared at her in blank shock, he watched fury spread across her face, blooming in two bright spots of color on her cheekbones. She looked down at the tangle of bandages in her hands, biting her lip.

Before he could stop himself—as he'd stopped himself over and over for twenty years—he started across the room toward her.

She turned, giving him a literal cold shoulder.

He wanted to stop. He didn't. He kept walking, through the beds with the wounded, until he reached her side.

"Go away." Her voice was low and fierce and infinitely beloved, melodious even in the depths of her weariness and anger. He hadn't heard it in twenty years, but it was as familiar to him as if he'd heard it this morning.

"Esme," he said, and touched her arm. She turned to look at him.

Her eyes ... there was a time when he'd lost himself in those eyes. They were green, shot through with gold. When he looked into her eyes, he used to sense the rustle of wings just over her shoulder; he used to see the wildness and glory of her dragon.

Now, they were merely the eyes of a woman, human to all outward appearance. But they were still very beautiful eyes.

They were also nearly black to the rims with fury.

"Will you let me explain?" he asked quietly.

"The time for explaining was twenty years ago."

He really couldn't argue with her there. He was also aware that they were starting to draw looks. Whatever this conversation was going to turn into, he couldn't have it with an audience.

"Esme, are you staying here in the Aerie? I can visit you later—"

"No," she whispered fiercely. The word came out in a hiss. "You may not. Now or ever."

There were a few silver threads squiggling through her heavy mass of red hair. She wore them unashamedly. Those were new, he thought. She was younger than he was, by nearly 200 years, but she hadn't had those twenty years ago.

He loved them, as he loved every part of her.

And there was nothing he could do about it.

But damned if he was going down without a fight.

"I am going hunting tomorrow with some of my guard, to

bring back fresh meat for those who are healing. You're welcome to join us, if you'd like."

She turned away from him, presenting her shapely shoulder to him, and went to check on one of the patients.

Well, he thought, that had actually gone much better than expected. She hadn't shifted into a dragon and tried to eat him. She hadn't thrown anything. She hadn't even raised her voice, although part of it, he was sure, was that Esme disliked a scene as much as she did. In private, it might have been a different matter.

Still, he thought, maybe there was hope.

Maybe, one of these days, he could get her to listen.

He didn't expect her to show up, but she was there, wearing a warm-looking green wool dress with a high collar that snugged right up to the bottom of her chin and a jacket over the top of it. If she was wearing it an attempt to make herself look unsexy, it didn't work. She would have looked sexy to him in a dress made from lampshades and traffic cones. Her hair was twisted into a thick red braid and wrapped around her head.

"Hunting, are we?" she declared with a raised brow. "Lead on, mighty hunter."

The flight of dragons shifted one by one, leaping into the air. Heikon led them, but he was very aware in his peripheral vision when Esme shifted. Her dragon was dazzling in the sun, still that same fresh leaf green, the same shade as her dress.

He hadn't hunted so terribly since he was a fledgling. He completely missed a dive at a deer exposed on a mountainside and nearly slammed into the trees. He failed to notice obvious prey on hillsides and mountaintops, only to have others dive past him to snatch mountain goats from clifftops or deer from meadows.

One by one, the rest of the dragons in his flight peeled off and flew back with their catches for the Aerie's kitchens. He and Esme were the last two remaining. It intrigued him that she hadn't taken a dive at any of the obvious game they'd seen. Surely she wasn't as distracted as he was.

Or was she?

A fat mountain sheep caught his eye on a ridge below. He folded his wings for a dive, only to have Esme flash past him, wings angled back for maximum speed.

Oh, that was how it was to be, was it?

He pulled up to let her take the prey. However, she merely swooped over without making contact with her claws. The sheep bolted for cover. Esme swooped upward and spread her wings to turn around and face him.

"What kind of chivalrous nonsense is this?" she demanded, her voice resonant and sibilant as it was reshaped by her powerful dragon's chest and the nonhuman throat and tongue. "You could have easily had that sheep!"

"You were already on it. I wasn't going to interfere."

"No, you wouldn't, would you?" she snarled, and turned with a hard flex of her wings and a huff. "Instead of us doing things side by side, it was always you doing it alone and leaving *me* alone, wasn't it? Why didn't I *see* it?"

"Esme!" It was torn from his throat in a snarl of frustration. "Esme, *listen*. I know you think I abandoned you. But I didn't dare contact you. I've been fighting for twenty years to get my clan back. The last thing I wanted to do was redirect my enemies toward you—"

"You could have asked me what *I* wanted!" she roared, and dived at him.

Startled, he winged to the side. Her charge missed and she spun around in midair. Heikon backbeat his wings and then folded them and dropped. He landed lightly on top of the ridge, shifting as his claws touched down so his weight settled on his boots instead.

It was simply too hard to have this conversation with Esme in a form where she could attack him.

But she didn't land. Instead she circled above him.

"Esme, come down here. Let's talk."

"We have nothing to say to each other," she declared from above. "I am going to finish this hunt and then leave, and I will never see you again. Do not contact me. All that there was between us was burned away twenty years ago."

The mate bond. He still shuddered to remember it.

Twenty years ago, Heikon's favorite place in the Aerie, other than the sakura grove, had been his study at the top of the mountain. It was at the pinnacle of the mountain, just above the lounge privately referred to as the Clubhouse where only Heikon and his elite warriors were allowed. From the walls of windows, he could look down upon all his lands and watch his clan going about their business, as safe and happy as he could make them.

He had never had a chance to bring Esme here. There was no time. Someday, he had thought then, when all of this unpleasant business with his brother was finished, he would bring her here.

And it would be finished soon, he hoped. A week, he'd promised Esme. Four days of that week were now elapsed. He'd received a brief phone call from her when she and Melody had landed in Greece, and a tightness in his chest had relaxed, knowing she was safely away. Meanwhile, Heikon had been keeping tabs on his brother Braun and the handful of Braun's co-conspirators that he'd identified so far.

It was understandable, he thought, for a younger brother to crave the power and prestige of a dragon clanlord. But Braun was really taking this too far. Maybe it would be necessary to lock him up for a decade or two in the dungeon beneath the mountain. If worst came to worst, he could challenge Braun to a duel in front of the entire clan. His brother was larger, but had always been a worse fighter due to his rashness and haste; Heikon was confident he could beat him. He just didn't really want to. They were brothers, after all.

But he really needed to do *something*. He shuffled the papers on his desk, the product of his private investigation. His brother could not be allowed to get away with this—

And then it happened.

A sudden, horrible weakness washed over him. His knees sagged and he collapsed into the chair behind his desk. His first, astonished thought was that he was having a heart attack. It almost felt like it. But then he realized that it was not his actual heart that was under attack, but the Heart of his hoard, the seat of every dragon's strength and power.

In the back of his mind, he felt a sudden surge of alarm that was not his own. Esme! All the way on the other side of the world, she had sensed that something was wrong.

He was able to lean on that bond for strength, slowly gathering himself again, with Esme's strength and courage providing a foundation beneath his own. He'd just risen to his feet, prepared to shift and go find out what was happening, when the door to his study burst in. At the same time, there was a thump against his window. He looked around in shock to see several dragons clinging to the railing outside his study, while his brother strode through the door at the head of a group of those Heikon had identified as the core of the conspiracy against him.

Heikon smiled fiercely, revealing teeth beginning to lengthen into fangs. They had done something dire to the

Heart of his hoard—he couldn't wait to make them pay for that—and now they expected to find him helpless. But with the mate bond to strengthen him, he couldn't lose.

Esme's alarm beat against the back of his mind. Between a dragon and its mate, the bond could sometimes be strong enough to allow two-way communication in times of great peril. He had always wondered if his would be that sort. Now he knew that it was.

Heikon! What's wrong?

Don't worry. It will be all right, he sent back, not knowing that those were the last words he would ever speak to her.

As Heikon threw himself into his shift, some of Braun's conspirators halted and began to fall back, realizing they were about to face not a weak and sick man, but a very angry dragon. There was room in the study for Heikon to transform, but no room in the hallway. He had, in fact, planned it that way. The advantage was his.

Only Braun looked unworried. Instead, his brother smiled thinly and said, "Goodbye, brother."

He made an overhand throwing motion.

Heikon finished his shift just as whatever it was, a tiny glass object, struck him in the snout and shattered.

There was a strange smell, almost odorless, a peculiar taste on the back of his tongue. He realized in an instant what it was, what it *had* to be, especially when Braun leaped quickly back and threw his arm across his face to keep from inhaling.

Concentrated essence of dragonsbane. A lethal poison to their kind, whether inhaled or absorbed through the skin.

Heikon threw himself backward, flinging his massive body into the window. The glass shattered, and the dragons gathered at the railing threw themselves out of the way rather than allowing themselves to become contaminated.

His head spun; his stomach rebelled. That much dragonsbane would kill him. Everything was failing: his ability to control his limbs, his connection to his dragon.

His connection to Esme.

He had to get it off. That was all he could think of. His wings carried him, somehow; he soared into the night, thinking of the many mountain lakes around the Aerie. He had to find one of them, dilute the poison, wash it off.

He couldn't feel Esme. All he could feel was the burning under his skin.

There was a lake ... there ...

He lost the ability to fly in midair. His wings gave out and he plummeted into dark water. It closed over his head, and he went down, down. The water was deep and cold, flooding his jaws, freezing his body.

It was the cold, he later thought, combined with near-lethal-but-not-quite levels of the drug, that must have helped him survive. Dragons in their shifted form were highly resilient and capable of slowing their metabolism to a near-hibernation state. Cases were known of dragons surviving incredible amounts of damage, living for years without food and water, and the like.

In this case, he sank to the bottom of the lake, into the mud, and there he lay as Braun's enforcers searched for him and eventually—though he would not learn of this until much later—decided he was dead.

It was pure survival instinct that made him crawl out. He only had flashes of that time; the first thing he remembered clearly was waking up in a grove of trees far from the lake, so weak he could barely move, sick and at the same time ravenously hungry, and with nothing, nothing at all in the back of his mind where Esme used to be.

"Esme," he whispered from a throat torn raw.

But she was gone.

The old stories said that a dose of dragonsbane just shy of lethal could sever the mate bond. Apparently it was true.

∾

W as everything that had been between them truly the mate bond and that alone? After all these years, did she really feel *nothing*?

"Esme!" he called, hoping she could still hear him. "The mate bond finds hearts that are compatible with each other. The most compatible. And even if the bond's not there ... *that's* still true, isn't it? All that we once had, all that we were to each other, hasn't changed."

Esme made no reply. Instead she circled higher.

"Esme!"

She folded her wings for a dive, and his heart lifted in hope. Was she coming down here? Instead, she swept out of sight over the ridge, rising moments later with the luckless mountain sheep gripped in her talons.

Heikon cursed under his breath. He shifted and sprang into the air, beating his powerful wings as he rose. By the time he achieved altitude, Esme was a small winged flicker in the blue bowl of the sky, headed for the Aerie.

Maybe she would listen, he thought. Best to give her a little time to cool off. He flew in a wide circle until he found prey of his own, a good-looking stag beside a pond. With the deer in his talons, he flew back home.

He got there to find that Esme had stayed only long enough to drop off her catch and gather her things. She was already gone.

ESME

From the large picture windows of her top-floor apartment, cup of cooling tea in hand, Esme watched rain and mist settle over the city. The dreary, rainy day suited her mood: gray and bleak.

Even after returning from Heikon's Aerie, she still couldn't get him out of her head. Damn that man.

All that we once had, all that we were to each other, hasn't changed, he'd had the nerve to say.

Oh, it changed, she thought furiously. *It changed when you shut me out in the most final way possible, by destroying our mate bond.*

He had thought he was protecting her; she understood that much. The fool, the idiot. And now they were nothing to each other.

You destroyed our mate bond and let me think you were dead for twenty years. No matter your reasons, that's how little I mean to you when it comes right down to it. What could possibly fix that?

Nothing. Nothing at all.

She took a sip from the teacup and found it had gone stone cold. If only dragons could really breathe fire, she thought with a grimace as she set her cup in the sink. She would never need a microwave again!

In the meantime, it was time to go downstairs and get ready for her evening ballroom dance class.

She pinned up her long red hair in front of the bathroom mirror, leaving the door open. The bathroom, like the rest of her apartment, was luxurious but not the kind of overt display of wealth that she had seen in many other dragons' homes, which she considered rather tasteless. She lived in a spacious, well-lit apartment that took up the entire top floor of the building, a renovated warehouse that she had purchased some time ago when the neighborhood was run-down, industrial, and cheap. More space than that, she neither needed nor wanted.

What could you think of a man who wanted to live in an entire mountain? Talk about overcompensating.

No, she preferred her apartment, with room to stretch out and live in, but not so much space that she'd rattle around like a ping-pong ball. Who wanted to live like Darius did, surrounded by gold-plated bathroom fixtures and antique rugs too expensive to step on?

And she loved the neighborhood, or rather, what the neighborhood had turned into. It had gone from being mostly warehouses, over the years, to a vibrant little arts community. Esme liked to think she'd had something to do with that; she had been quietly investing in businesses throughout the neighborhood ever since remodeling the warehouse into a living and working space and moving in.

She loved living somewhere that she only had to walk two shopfronts down the street to buy bread from a lovely little French bakery, and two more shopfronts took her to an old-fashioned greengrocer. There were restaurants and art galleries and all manner of art studios within easy walking distance. All the business owners knew her and greeted her by name.

Try explaining that to other dragons, though.

Every dragon had their own distinctive quirks, but Esme's fondness for city life was very unusual. Most dragons preferred solitude and isolation—mountain fortresses, hidden caves. Heikon's Aerie was the rule rather than the exception. Esme's own clan dwelt in an assortment of private chalets high in the mountains in Switzerland.

But Esme loved the glitter and excitement of city life. She loved being exposed to new kinds of music and new technology for making music.

And, her secret shame as a dragon: she really liked humans, too.

Other dragons might tolerate humans as servants, rarely even take them as mates. But dragons weren't *friends* with humans. They didn't live among them and enjoy their company.

Esme did.

It was a lonely life, sometimes. From their point of view, she didn't age, so she had made travel a part of her life, moving from one home to another and never staying in one place for more than a couple of decades. Some rare friends were let in on her secret, but the community must never learn. So the butchers and grocers whose shops she visited, the patrons of the cafés where she went to sip coffee and listen to bands play, the local musicians she got to know: all of these were left behind each time she went on to a new place.

She had chosen to view it as a series of opportunities, not losses. She'd lived in Vienna and Paris and New York; she'd also lived in a series of small, no-name cities around the world, enjoying the cultural and social opportunities they had to offer. Usually she divided her time between a few different homes scattered across the world—and the Heart of her hoard, of course, the place where no one had ever been except Esme herself.

When she bought this building, it was only an investment —by now she'd gotten good at recognizing neighborhoods where property values were likely to go up, buying cheap and renting them out for reasonable rates as the neighborhoods improved around them. But once she was done renovating it, she liked it so much that she had decided to move in.

And it had been her salvation in the last twenty years, as she suffered the agony of the broken mate bond, the grief of knowing she had lost her mate before she even got to know him. Without the building renovations to throw herself into, without the community surrounding her, she didn't know how she would have survived.

And now he thinks he can come waltzing back into my life as if those twenty years never happened. As if we're still mates.

Fury sparked green and gold in her eyes in the mirror, brief flashes of the dragon inside her.

How very presumptive of him, her dragon agreed. *As if he thinks he is our mate. We have no mate!*

She turned away with a soft hissing growl, before she could give in to the urge to shift and go flying. This dim gray weather was the only sort of weather in which a city dragon could fly in the daytime, and it was very tempting to take advantage of it ... but no, she lost track of time easily when she was a dragon, and she didn't want to disappoint her evening dance class.

She clipped on a pair of emerald and gold earrings, matching her green dress, and slipped into her dancing shoes. And now the best part: choosing the music.

Feeling a little more buoyant and less depressed, she

tripped down the stairs to the middle floor of the renovated warehouse.

When she had done the remodeling, she'd lavished attention on the top floor—her apartment—and the bottom floor, which was a combination dance studio and community space. But in between was a level that was only for her, and it was where she kept her hoard.

All dragons hoarded in their own unique way. Esme's hoard was music.

The second floor of the warehouse housed a collection of records, tapes, CDs, and other storage media that would have made many a museum curator envious. She had records in pristine condition going all the way back to the earliest wax cylinders. She had bought most of them when they were new, played them a few times, and then put them away; there was always something new to listen to, and she preferred live music anyway, but somehow could never resist her urge to collect it.

That was, after all, what it meant to be a dragon. You hoarded things.

In addition to the commercial recordings, she also owned bootlegs of thousands of concerts, most of them one of a kind. As she brushed her fingers across the edge of each slipcover, she heard, in her mind, the music it contained, and felt her steps pick up, moving gracefully as if in the steps of a private dance.

This was only a fraction of her true hoard, of course. Esme not only had other warehouses full of records and CDs, but she had leaped into the world of digital music with absolute delight. She had been thrilled to discover that entire rooms full of records could be stored on a single hard drive of MP3s. Her collection of live bootleg recordings had also grown by leaps and bounds now that every concertgoer was equipped with a cell phone. Of course, she still liked having the physical objects; for a dragon, there was no substitute for being able to hold treasures from your hoard in your hands. But ... you could just have so much music in digital storage. *So much.* It made her dragon want to roll around with glee.

There was also a fully equipped recording studio on this floor, with soundproofed walls and state-of-the-art equipment; she peeked inside as she went past, just to enjoy it. Her hoard did not consist only of music recordings; in fact, she sometimes considered those the lesser part of it. She owned several small recording labels and enjoyed personally talent-scouting at musical competitions, bars, small outdoor concerts, and other places where new talent could be found. She also invested in symphonies and music schools.

And she loved to teach.

Not as a teacher of music. For all that Esme hoarded music, *creating* it was not really her thing. She could sing competently, but all the times she'd tried to learn an instrument—and during a couple hundred years of a dragon's lifespan, she'd tried a number of them—had only frustrated her. Esme could recognize true musical genius, and she didn't have it. She enjoyed playing the piano and other instruments (there were a number of different instruments in the apartment) but only for her own pleasure, not as a performance for others.

But teaching people to dance was perfectly suited to Esme's talents and disposition. She *loved* spinning around the room to beautiful music, showing other people how to let the music flow through them as it was meant to be experienced. Selecting a different part of her music collection for each dance lesson was her special joy. Dragons who hoarded gold and jewels might cling to them jealously, but music was meant to be listened to and shared. A record that was never played was just a circular piece of vinyl. Music was at its best when played out loud in a big venue with good acoustics, with a bunch of people dancing to it.

She selected a stack of records and CDs, and went down to the ballroom. Her dancing shoes clicked on the floor, echoing through the large, empty room. The last people who'd used it were the AA group that met at noon, and they had stacked the chairs neatly out of the way, as she had asked them to. She checked the sound system and got the music ready.

And all the while, she tried very hard not to think about Heikon twirling her around the ballroom, his hand strong and warm in the small of her back. It was a foolish fantasy, she told herself firmly—but she realized she'd been unconsciously fitting her steps to those of an invisible partner as she moved around the room, skimming and gliding, as if in response to someone else's steps.

Foolish. Pointless.

All of that was over, and it was never coming back.

HEIKON

"You're going to follow her and spy on her? That'll end well, I'm sure."

"I am not *spying*," Heikon said with all the dignity he could muster. "I am going to approach her on ground on which she has the advantage and *talk* to her. Neutrally, with no strings attached. Which of these jackets do you prefer, the dark red or the emerald?"

Reive merely rolled his eyes at him. Heikon's great-nephew was a young dragon, still very close to the age he appeared to be in human terms; he looked in his late 20s and was only a few years older than that in reality.

Sarcasm, Heikon mused, was not an appealing trait in the young.

"Fine, the dark red jacket it is," he decided, pulling it over the crisp black shirt he'd already selected.

"Good choice," Reive said. "It won't show the blood when she bites you in the face."

"Don't you have somewhere to be?"

"But this is so much more fun."

Heikon growled at him. Reive actually laughed, brightening his sharp, handsome features for a moment, as he slipped out of Heikon's chambers.

It had been a pleasure to watch life in the Aerie return to normal after Heikon had reclaimed his seat from his brother two years ago. At first the place had been gloomy and dark. The entire family had lived in fear of Braun's sudden rages, had worried about even so much as mentioning Heikon's name for fear of being branded traitors and imprisoned or worse. The younger members of the family had never known anything else, and those like Reive, who Heikon remembered as happy, laughing children, had grown up into wary adults, forever looking over their shoulder for a betrayal or a punishment.

Restoring life in the mountain to all that it used to be had been his duty and his pleasure over the last two years.

But now he was starting to realize there was something else—*someone* else ... another duty, another pleasure, never far from his mind for all that time, but ...

But she doesn't know that.

Esme had no idea how often he'd dreamed of her, how he'd denied himself and waited, waited, knowing that he didn't dare bring her back into his life until it was safe for her.

And then went on denying himself, making excuses, telling himself that he couldn't bring her back to the Aerie when it was a dark and gloomy place still recovering from twenty years of Braun's rule.

And then the time slips away, and you realize what a mistake you've made, once it's too late to recover from it ...

He looked at himself in the mirror, pulling the shoulders of the jacket straight, twitching at its lapels, and finally admitted to himself that he was stalling.

Just as he'd been stalling for years, not wanting to hear

33

from Esme's own lips that she no longer wanted him without the bond.

She must have thought him dead. He'd let his clan believe him so, and Esme must have believed it too. Had she searched for him? He wasn't sure what hurt more, that she'd held onto the faith and tried to find him during the years he was living in exile—or that she had simply moved on, found other loves and other things to fill her time.

Had it filled her with joy, when she learned he was alive, that Braun's poison had been nonfatal? If so, it didn't show now.

For of course, his brother's poison had killed the best part of both of them.

Maybe she blamed him for Braun's actions. Maybe after all this time, she thought he was as responsible for the civil war within his clan as Braun was.

Maybe she was right. If he'd listened more, defused the tension with his brother before it erupted into an outright assassination attempt, none of this had to happen.

Is there still hope for us, Esme?

Not if he didn't fight for her, for *them*. And with that thought, he went out onto the balcony of his chambers in the Aerie.

Below him, the mountainside rolled downward, a tapestry of meadows and garden terraces and patches of forest. Much of the damage from the fighting in the gargoyle war had been cleaned up now, and it warmed the aching places in his heart to see the mountain's former beauty blossoming again. As he scanned the slopes with his sharp eyes, he located various members of his clan—his family— enjoying the warm day, working in the gardens or playing or sunning themselves in dragon form.

Long ago, he had dreamed of this place as a safe haven, a place where young dragon children could grow up without worrying about humans—where they could be themselves, far away from the prying eyes of the human world. And now it was becoming that again, slowly but surely.

He stepped off the balcony and shifted as he went: a huge dragon, glossy gunmetal blue, sheened with silver.

Below him, various members of his clan looked up and waved as he flew over. A small group of teenage dragons jumped off a ledge where they had been lying in the sun, and kept up with him for a little while, flying around him in a flashing swirl of green and purple and golden wings before they turned back and swirled down to the forest below.

Heikon kept flying until he left his lands behind. Cloudy weather closed in around him, low gray clouds and mist providing cover from the ground. Which was just as well, because now he was passing over scattered houses and the dots of grazing sheep and cattle far below.

Rural farm and ranch country gave way, eventually, to small towns and then suburbs, glimpsed through the clouds. Heikon's wings were feeling the strain now, but in a pleasant way, the good ache of a satisfying workout. It had been a while since he'd been on a long flight.

We should hunt, his dragon said, stirring lazily in his mind. It had been content for some time now, completely present within its own skin, thinking of nothing but the stretch of too-long-unused muscles, the rush of the wind and the pleasantly cool flow of occasional bursts of rain over his scales.

Not now. We seek our mate.

We have no mate. The dragon's reply was not upset so much as merely confused.

Rather than start that argument all over again, Heikon folded his wings and dived into the clouds. He was flying over the city now, so he had to be careful; there was more air traffic up here, and also a much greater chance of being spotted when he dipped low in the clouds to get his bearings.

35

On the bright side, city people didn't look up that much, and when they did, they were more likely to think, "Hmm, big jet" rather than "Dragon!"

He had known of Esme's residence in the city for some time now, but had never been there. He approached it by flying low over the docks and then weaving his way through a mostly-deserted warehouse district. When the lights of small businesses began to appear below him, gleaming through the rainy dusk, he touched down in a dark spot between a fence and a malfunctioning street light, and shifted. Four hundred years gave him a lot of practice at doing it quickly and stealthily; he folded his wings and was human by the time his now-shod feet lightly touched the ground. Anyone watching would have seen little more than shadows and perhaps a flash of blue scales.

He stretched his arms to ease the ache of rearranged muscles, and adjusted his jacket, smoothed his hair to the side. His hand came away damp. Right ... it was raining here, a soft, steady drizzle.

It occurred to him that he should probably have brought an umbrella.

But there were human stores around. Useful. He stopped into three stores asking for umbrellas, and finally found a store that had just one left, which he bought. He didn't realize until he'd stepped out onto the street and opened it that it was covered in bright green frogs.

Heikon sighed. Perhaps it was for the best? Esme liked green, after all. He could tell her that it was in her honor.

He should have worn the emerald jacket. Too late now.

The umbrella was ever so slightly too small for a man his size, and occasionally dripped cold rainwater down his collar. It was a mystery for the ages, Heikon thought as he gloomily made his way down the street, that rain felt so very nice on his dragon's scales, and so *unpleasant* when it was making his human clothes cling to his skin.

We could be a dragon again, his dragon suggested hopefully.

Not here we can't.

His dragon, which had absolutely no comprehension of cars, people, or witnesses, subsided with sulky ill grace.

He took a wrong turn and had to ask directions from a woman who was just closing an art gallery, but she knew exactly who he meant when he mentioned Esme, and a few minutes later he was standing across the street from a building that looked exactly like what it was: a converted warehouse. It was a big square block of a building, dominating its side of the street. Heikon's soul, soothed by meadows and gardens, shrank from the unnatural squareness and ugliness of it. In his mountain, everything was smooth curves and natural stone. Surely she couldn't *enjoy* living in a place like that, shut away from the wild world in a manner that was completely unnatural for dragons.

She must have shut herself up and walled away the world in her grief, Heikon mused. The square prison-like shape of the building reflected the bleakness in her soul.

How could he have stayed away from her for so many years, leaving her to *this*?

Are we going to be here long? his dragon asked. *I'm bored. I thought we were flying.*

We're here on a very important mission.

Does it involve fat sheep?

He decided not to dignify that with a response, and crossed the street.

The building looked less bleak up close ... somewhat, at least. Rather than painting over the brick, it had been finished in a way that made the brick look sharp and new, with crisp trim. There were large windows on the top floor, and also the ground floor, looking out on the street. Some of them showed what appeared to be empty conference rooms, but several were lit up with warm lamplight within. Floor-to-ceiling vertical blinds concealed most of what was going on inside, but when he looked in, he realized that all the lamplit windows belonged to the same large interior space, a sort of ballroom or dance hall.

And there were dancers.

He spotted Esme immediately, of course. She was the only one not paired with a partner, but she still moved in rhythm to the music he couldn't hear from outside. She waltzed alone, gracefully and silently dancing from one person to the next. She did not intrude, merely touched a shoulder here, an arm there, correcting her dancers with small brushes of her hands.

She wore a green dress with a knee-length skirt that flared around her as she moved. Her vivid red hair was piled on her head, held up with pins that looked like they were barely containing the living mass of it, as if pulling out a single pin could send it all tumbling over her shoulders. How well he remembered the feeling of it spilling through his hands; twenty years was but a moment. He could have touched her yesterday, so well did his hands remember the feeling of her hair, the supple smoothness of her skin ...

Bored, his dragon announced.

Shut up!

He had forgotten how Esme dominated a room. As she gracefully waltzed from one dancer to another, there was no way that the eye could not be drawn to her. Every line of her body was grace and beauty ... and joy. When she turned so that he could glimpse her face, her eyes were half closed and she appeared to be lost in the music, lips parted and sweet bliss on her face.

He'd never seen a woman who looked less bleak and miserable in his life.

She puts on a brave face, he thought, and his heart broke with love for her strength and resilience.

We could be hunting right now, you know, his dragon suggested.

Quiet, reptile, that's our mate in there.

No it's not, his dragon reported after a quick look.

His dragon might not know her, with the mate bond broken between them. But *he* would. He would know her in darkness or sunshine, would know her as a dragon or a human. He would know her dancing alone, or in a crowded room, or ...

Er. Or staring through the window, as she was now doing, with a decidedly unfriendly look on her face.

ESME

Tonight Esme had most of her regulars for the evening seniors' ballroom dance class. Miriam, perched birdlike in her wheelchair, never missed a class. Albert and Greta had turned up this time, married for 55 years and so completely lost in each other, even in their late 70s, that she had her hands full trying to get them to dance with anyone else. The one and only unattached man in the class—George, a rather shy 80-something who wore his high-waisted pants with suspenders—had been instantly claimed as a dance partner by one of the single women, Lupe. This just left Judy, hair spiked up in a bristling gray bush and wearing jeans rather than a skirt as most of the female seniors preferred. As usual, she looked a little awkward on the dance floor, like she felt that she didn't quite fit; at 69, she was the youngest person in the seniors class, and preferred to dance the male parts.

"Dance with me, dear?" Miriam asked, her wrinkled face creased with smiles, holding out her hands.

Judy smiled and took her hands gently. "I'd love to dance with you."

When Miriam had joined the class, Esme had looked up videos on Youtube of how to dance with people in wheel-chairs. By now she had taught this to most of her regulars, with Miriam as their partner, and so Judy knew just what to do; she led in the dance, gently pulling Miriam around through the steps.

Esme started out with a Strauss waltz, and moved briskly around her students, for the most part letting them dance on their own; none of her beginning students were here tonight, and this bunch came here mainly for the dance practice and camaraderie. Greta had brought a coffee cake, and a stack of pretty little plates, to go with the coffee Esme always laid out. (Expensive French roast, of course; no cheap bargain-base-ment coffee for *her* students.) By now the students knew each other, and enjoyed renewing their acquaintance.

Esme danced in between the couples, moving with the music, and feeling, all the while, the cold lack of a partner to dance with. It wouldn't have mattered if she cut in and danced with someone, with Miriam or Judy or even George —what she was missing was *her* partner, the one who would have completed her. It was all the more painful for having thought she had found that, and then lost it.

How could two people seem to fit so perfectly, only for it all to go wrong?

And then she opened her eyes, having let them drift shut as she flowed along with the music, and found herself looking toward the window, out into the darkened street—at Heikon.

Esme stopped moving, freezing in place in the middle of the dance floor. He was standing there looking at her through the window, holding a ludicrous plastic umbrella with cartoon frogs on it, which he had allowed to slip down to his shoulder; his hair was getting wet.

As she continued to stare, he turned away—and a part of

her wanted to shout at him to stop, to stay ... until she realized that he was *not* leaving, but rather, heading for the door.

Oh no!

She dashed toward the door in a flurry of clicking heels, but he had already opened it before she could get there and slam the lock home. He stepped inside, shaking off the umbrella, and Esme clattered to a stop.

"Hi," he said, a bit sheepishly, and smiled at her.

The rain humanized him, made him seem less like a regal dragonlord and more like a middle-aged man who had been caught out in a cloudburst. The shoulders of his ludicrous brick-red dinner jacket were dark with water—and honestly, what did he think he was dressing up for, a mobster's wedding? The rain darkened his salt-and-pepper hair, glistened on his smooth bronze skin. She wouldn't mind licking it off—

Why are we wasting time with a man who broke our heart? her dragon complained. *There is music! Dancing!*

Too right. Esme firmly got herself under control and folded her arms. She was not affected in the *slightest* by the way he was looking at her, the smile that still melted her, the dark eyes full of tentative hope.

Behind her, she was conscious of the dancers clattering and in one case rolling to a stop as they became aware that something was going on.

"As you can see, I'm in the middle of a class," she said. "Say what you came to say and leave."

His smile faltered. "Yes, a class," he said. "Right. You ... teach classes?"

So little he knew about her ... or her about him. Perhaps it was never meant to last no matter what.

"Yes," she said sharply, "and I need to get back to—"

"Oh, Esme dear, who is this handsome man?" Miriam's

cracked voice said, and Esme could have sunk through the floor. "Do we have another *male* student?"

Esme could not quite understand how it happened, but her students surrounded Heikon and swept him into the room, showing him where to leave his umbrella, giving him a towel. They had always been friendly with new people; normally she encouraged it. Now she was so caught off guard that she failed to put a stop to it until it was too late.

"There's coffee cake!" Greta exclaimed. "Have some. It's my mother's recipe."

"And the coffee is excellent," Lupe put in.

"Eat up, dear, you look like you need it," Miriam quavered.

"A ... student," Heikon said, standing with a plate of coffee cake in one hand, a plastic fork in the other, and looking vaguely boggled and confused in a way that was most certainly *not* adorable. "Can I ... er ... sign up for your class?"

"Oh, that would be wonderful!" Greta cried, clapping her hands. "There are never enough dancers to take the male parts; my Albert prefers to dance with me, of course, and other than that we just have George ... oh, and there's Judy—no offense, Judy—"

"None taken," Judy sighed.

How, Esme thought in dismay. *How did this happen?!* And now she had no idea how to back out gracefully in front of the students. She looked into Heikon's face and saw all of a sudden, in her mind's eye, how deeply she could hurt him in return; she could fly at him like the dragon that she was, rending and tearing with words, cutting him to the bone just as he had cut her; she could tell everyone exactly what he'd done, that he'd broken her heart, abandoned her. She could tear him down so completely that her students would want nothing to do with him!

And then she saw from the mildly quizzical look that he

cast at the students that he wouldn't care. Oh, he would care about the words she said to him ... probably. Maybe. But it didn't matter to him if she did it in front of the students or not. He was a typical dragon; humans as individuals were meaningless to him, useful only in what they could do for him.

But what if I could make you care? she thought, looking at him with her head tilted to the side. *What if I could make you see them as I see them? Show you how to like them? And then reveal to them who you really are and pull the rug out from under your feet!*

She was vaguely aware on some level that this was a ridiculously convoluted revenge plan, but her dragon was highly approving. *Does it mean that we get to dance and also bite him?*

Yes! Esme thought back, and she said, "Can you dance at all?"

"Not well," Heikon said, and the tentative smile grew bolder. "That's why I need you to teach me."

Oh, *that* smile. Not his apology smile, but his infuriating and even more panty-melting smile of absolute confidence, the smile that said he thought he was winning.

We'll just see about that.

"Yes," she said, smiling back at him, showing some teeth. "Of course. In fact, why don't we get back to it."

The record had stopped playing. She went and switched to another, taking her time putting it on, asking herself the entire time what on earth she thought she was doing.

It's only one class, she thought. *I can make him leave anytime I want.*

The sweet strains of music filled the dance hall. Esme closed her eyes for a moment, enjoying it, and then she turned back ... to find that the couples had already paired up again, leaving Heikon and herself the only ones unpaired.

Oops.

She looked around hastily, wondering if she could break up any of the dancing pairs. Albert and Greta were .... well ... no. Miriam was always happy to dance with anyone who wanted to, but she and Judy seemed to be having fun tonight, and Esme felt bad about breaking them up; it was always so hard to get Judy involved in the class activities. And Miriam was a challenging partner because of the wheelchair.

Esme heaved a deep sigh and threw herself on that grenade for the sake of her class.

"Let's get this over with," she snapped, and held out a hand to Heikon.

"And a more charming invitation I couldn't imagine," he said, taking her hand.

She was unprepared for her own reaction to the feeling of his skin on hers. His fingers were slightly callused, warm and strong. Her hand fit into his as if it was meant to be there.

With a tentativeness that she didn't expect from him, he carefully settled his other hand at the small of her back. It rested there very lightly, hardly even touching the silky fabric of her dress, as if he was nervous to hold her too closely for fear that he might cause her to slip away.

She was shocked to feel a slight tremor in the fingers holding her own, as if he was as uncertain about this—as nervous—as she was.

Almost against her will, Esme looked up at his face. She hadn't been this close to him in twenty years, and she was hyper-aware of his body so near to hers; it seemed as if she could feel the warmth of his entire body, even though nothing touched her but his hands.

And he was looking down at her with the full depth of twenty years' longing in his eyes.

Her whole body seemed to tingle. She was frozen, hardly hearing the music.

This wasn't going to work at all.

She jerked her hand out of his, and glided out of his grasp, taking a few steps back until she regained some distance and, with it, her composure. She was gasping as if she'd just run a mile. Her heart raced.

She couldn't do this. She couldn't spin around the room on this man's arm and pretend to feel nothing. Her resistance would crumble, she *knew* it would.

How could he still have this much of an effect on her? The mate bond was broken! They were nothing to each other now. She should be able to touch him, to look into his eyes, and feel nothing.

"I think we've had enough waltzing for now," she said in a voice pitched to carry across the room. "Why don't we switch to swing dancing for awhile?"

There. That should be good: a nice, active, and most importantly *unpartnered* dance. Or at least one that did not require dancing very closely in intimate proximity with anyone. She very nearly fled the room to go get some jazz records.

Once the lively strains filled the ballroom, things relaxed a bit. Soon the entire class were dancing vigorously— including Heikon. He clearly had absolutely no idea what he was doing, but the other ladies in the class were eager to show him.

Hot, vicious jealousy washed over Esme, shocking her.

What's the matter with me? With shaking hands, she fussed with the coffee things, turning her back on her gaily dancing students. *He is nothing to me. What do I care if he dances with other women? Human women, at that!*

But she looked over her shoulder and saw a laughing Lupe correcting his dance steps, and for an instant she was seized with an overwhelming urge to shift into a dragon and scare that woman away from her m—

He's not our mate!

I know!

The evening passed in a haze of jealousy and longing. For the first time, Esme was deeply glad when they reached the end of the class period and everyone began to break up and drift out. Esme began packing up the coffee things. Heikon lingered.

"Do you want something?" she asked shortly.

She made the mistake of looking up as she said it. Without meaning to, she caught his eyes, and she saw her answer there. *You. Forever. Always.*

She tore her gaze away, and picked up two coffee cups with a hand that trembled so hard that the cups clinked together.

She ought to make him leave. There was no good reason to let him stay. Her revenge plan had been utterly foolish. The only person she had trapped was herself.

Instead, she thrust the cups at him. "You can wash these. Have you ever washed a dish in your life?"

"I do know the technique," he said solemnly.

There was a break room downstairs so that she didn't have to run up and down three flights of stairs with the coffee things and other refreshments, so she left him there, washing dishes, while she went to put the records away. Occasionally she could hear soft clinking and the sound of running water. It was oddly companionable, a feeling she could have easily relaxed into, if she hadn't had to keep reminding herself not to.

It was just ... *strange*, having him casually in her space in such a domestic way. They had never done anything like this before. Their courtship had been a dazzling, romantic whirl-wind of moonlight trysts and hot sex. She had looked back on it as the great love of her life, and only now realized that they'd never really gotten to do any normal couple things.

They'd never cooked together, or lounged around in pajamas reading books with their feet tangled together, or argued over whose turn it was to clean the bathroom, or ...

Her eyes filled with tears. She fiercely blinked them away, realized she'd misfiled a record, and slipped it carefully into its proper slot.

And they would never do any of those things, because they were no longer mates and were never going to be. Play-acting at it now would only hurt both of them.

She marched into the break room with fierce, renewed determination to simply throw him out. And then she was brought up short at the actual sight of him, shirtsleeves rolled up, dish suds on his arms, head bent as he diligently dried a mug on a dish towel.

It was not precisely *sexy* (although, she had to face it, Heikon couldn't stop being sexy if he tried) as it was vulnerable. In this moment he was not the dragon clanlord; he was just a man, and she had the feeling that very few people had ever seen him like this.

She broke the moment by clearing her throat.

Heikon looked up, and a warm smile spread across his face; it was all she could do not to respond in kind. He let the water out of the sink and carefully wiped around the edges of it with the towel. "Dishes are done," he said. "Do you have any other tasks for me?"

Once again, her nice, tidy train of thought derailed. "What? I'm not—what do you think this is, one of those fairy tales where I give you three impossible tasks and you complete them and I take you back?"

His smile returned, touched with a hint of play. "If that's what we're doing, you're going to have to make the next one a lot harder."

"It's not what we're doing!"

The playful look faded, and she was instantly sorry. She bit her lip to stop herself from saying anything.

And then she did think of something.

One of the toilets in the downstairs public rest rooms was out of order. She'd been meaning to call a plumber about it, but with one thing and another kept forgetting to do it during business hours.

So he wanted to help out, did he.

"How are you at fixing toilets?" she asked sweetly.

Heikon stared at her, as if the words hadn't registered. "I'm sorry?" he said after a moment.

"Toilets. We have a broken toilet. I need someone to fix it. Do you think you can do that without breaking it even more badly?"

Heikon cleared his throat. "I was thinking, er ... catching you a rare sort of antelope, bringing back a special flower from a distant mountain, that sort of thing."

"You wanted to help. I have something you can do to help. Of course," she added, "if you're no good with toilets, I can call someone. Or just do it myself."

That had an effect, as she'd hoped. "No, no, of course I can do it," Heikon said, sounding none too sure about that.

Heikon caught completely off guard was ... definitely not adorable in the slightest. She wasn't even going to think it.

"This way, then," she said, managing to keep her smile on the inside, for the most part. "I'll show you where the tools are."

HEIKON

This was *impossible*. How did people do this kind of thing? Normal humans, even!

Heikon had gotten himself through the process of dismantling the toilet by reminding himself that small, weak humans took toilets apart every day, so certainly a dragon could do it. It wasn't even a disgusting process. He'd had visions of ... well ... something far worse than this, but the actual problem (Esme had explained) was just that the toilet kept running all the time, wasting water, so she'd shut off the water to it and marked the stall out of order.

"I think it's probably just a matter of replacing a gasket," she'd said matter-of-factly after showing him to the broken toilet and handing him a toolbox. "I just haven't gotten around to tearing it down to find out. If I don't have the right parts to fix it, let me know and I'll order them."

Heikon was still trying to wrap his head around the idea of his elegant, stylish mate fixing toilets. Fortunately he had managed not to say so—she would probably have whomped him in the head with one of the wrenches in the toolbox—

but from the withering look she gave him, she had apparently read it on his face anyway.

"It's amazing the things you learn how to do when there's no one around to help you with it," she'd said, and stomped off.

So here he was with a mostly dismantled toilet and a strong suspicion that going and asking her for help would constitute failure.

We could be out hunting, his dragon grumbled.

Unless you're going to tell me how to fix this, shut up.

He'd taken off his suit jacket and slung it over the top of the stall, but even so he had a feeling that these clothes were never going to be the same again. It wasn't that things were filthy, exactly—at least not as much so as he had imagined. Actually, Esme's restrooms were very clean and tidy, as these things went. Still, he couldn't believe he was on his knees in a human restroom, wrestling with a toilet.

He held up a rubber piece, as if staring at it could help him figure out what it did. How did he get himself into these things? How did toilets even *work*?

Maybe he could just ... call a plumber and not tell her. Yes, that was a good idea.

Except she would almost certainly find out, and then she'd think even less of him than she already did, if that was possible.

Perhaps he could call someone. Someone who might know how to fix toilets. Someone in the Aerie must know, surely. One of the younger members of the family, the ones who had been raised in an era with indoor plumbing. Someone who would be discreet and trustworthy.

He stuck his head out of the stall to make sure Esme wasn't lingering around to hear this, and then called Reive.

"Uncle!" Reive said in surprise. There was the sound of childish giggling in the background; Reive must be babysitting some of the clan children at the moment. He'd always been good with them. "Will you be back to the Aerie tonight?"

"Probably not," Heikon said, gazing at the scatter of toilet parts spread around him. "Do you ... er ... know anything about fixing toilets?"

There was a long silence. "Toilets," Reive said.

"Yes."

"How on Earth did you go from wooing your mate to *that?*"

"I am impressing her by fixing her toilet."

It was obvious from Reive's tone that he was trying not to laugh. "The fact that you're calling me to ask for help would suggest it's not going well."

"It's going perfectly well," Heikon said defensively. "Aside from a few minor issues."

"Such as?"

Such as having no idea what I'm doing. "Do you know how to fix a toilet or not? I assume it's a skill of the young."

"Have you tried Google?"

"If I wanted to use the Googles, I would have used the Googles," Heikon snapped, refusing to admit that while he had vaguely heard of these Googles, he had never used them and wasn't entirely sure how.

There was a slight choking sound on the other end of the line. "Okay," Reive said after a minute, taking a deep breath that had only the slightest hitch in it. "I'll text you some pictures, okay?"

"I knew you were the one to ask," Heikon said.

"Though it would help if you'd tell me exactly what's wrong."

"If I knew what was wrong, I wouldn't have had to call you."

Another brief silence, and then Reive said, "Hang on. I'll call you back."

With that, he ended the call.

"You can't just hang up on your clanlord, boy!" Heikon snapped at the phone.

He heard the clicking of Esme's heels just in time to put down the phone, pick up the wrench, and try to look like he was doing something useful.

"How's it going in here?" Esme said, poking her head into the stall.

"Oh, perfectly well, thank you." Heikon gave the wrench a casual twist on whatever it was currently attached to. There was a clunk. He hoped that wasn't bad. "As you can see, I'm quite busy. Fixing your toilet."

"So I see," Esme said wryly. "Well ... I've finished setting up for tomorrow's classes, so I'm going upstairs to my apartment. Though I could wait down here if you're not going to be long. Do you expect to be much longer?"

"No, of course not," Heikon said, and then the part of the pipe he'd hooked the wrench onto fell off. "Er ... perhaps just a little bit longer."

"Yes," she said, the corners of her mouth dimpling briefly before it flattened out with a determined air. "In that case ..." She hesitated for a moment, then held out her hand with a small piece of paper clutched between her fingers. "I'm going to lock up, but this is the security code to the outside doors. Punch the code into the keypad by the door, and then you have thirty seconds to open the door or it'll re-arm."

Her fingers brushed over his, warm and soft, as he took it from her. A gesture of trust, he thought. That meant something, didn't it?

For a bare instant longer, after the paper left her fingers, her hand continued to hang in the air, as if she wanted to reach after it and take his hand again. Then she pulled it back with a certain air of decisive firmness, as if reining herself in. "And turn off the lights when you leave," she said, and turned on her heel and strode out with quick, clicking steps.

Going upstairs. To her apartment.

He firmly attempted to eject any and all thoughts of Esme in her apartment. And yet, it was impossible not to picture her, as if their connection of twenty years ago had left him with the ability to *feel* her—as if he could feel the distance between them stretching out again, step by step. He told himself it was his imagination; even the mate bond was not quite that precise. And yet, he could see her, in his mind's eye. Walking up the stairs. Opening the door. Perhaps taking off her shoes, perhaps pouring herself a glass of wine. He couldn't quite picture the surroundings, but he could picture her, pulling out the pins holding up her long hair so it could tumble down her back—the way it used to tumble when he would unpin it in the Aerie, long red-gold waves spilling through his hands—

It was probably just as well his phone interrupted his fantasies at that moment. It was Reive calling back.

"Okay, Uncle, did you get the text I sent you?"

"Yes," Heikon said promptly, and fumbled with his phone trying to figure out how to get to the texts without hanging up. For some reason Reive had texted him a picture of an incomprehensible pile of ... no wait, that was a toilet, partly dismantled.

"Go ahead and put the phone on speaker so we can talk while you do this," Reive said.

"Are you ... taking apart one of the toilets in the Aerie?"

"Yes," Reive said, "so let's finish this quickly, before Aunt Anjelica comes in and sees what I'm doing." There was a high-pitched childish giggle in the background. "No, Feo, go play with your sister. Ow! No, not that—okay, hold this for me, will you?"

Now it was Heikon's turn to try not to laugh. "Sounds like you have help."

"Tell me about it. Just a second, I'll give you a picture."

Another text came in a minute later. There was a chubby little boy with dark curls clutching a wrench in his hand, and a tiny pink and gold dragon crawling up onto the toilet tank: Feodran and his sister Pixie. They were Reive's cousins once or twice removed; at this point Heikon almost needed a scorepad and paper to work out the various relationships between his ever-growing clan of grandkids and grand-nieces/nephews and their cousins and their cousins' cousins and so forth.

"Anyway," Reive said, "I've got things pulled apart, as you can see, so I can walk you through the repairs you need to do. Go ahead and text me a picture of what's happening on your end."

Heikon fumbled with the phone again, thinking as he did so that this modern technology was hard to use, but really kind of useful.

～

He wasn't sure, in the end, exactly how long it took, and there was a pause halfway through when Reive had to go put two sleepy little dragons to bed, but eventually there was a neatly reconstructed toilet in front of him. It flushed. It didn't leak. It looked perfect.

"Thank you," Heikon said sincerely.

"Anything I can do to help out the clanlord, right?"

They had ended up using a video chat app—Reive had walked Heikon through this, too—so they could see what each other were doing without having to send pictures back and forth. Which meant that Heikon could see Reive now, sleepy-looking and relaxed, sitting on the bathroom floor with his back against the wall. When Reive had taken a break to put the kids away, he'd also grabbed a beer; it was beside him on the floor, half empty.

"It's a lot better than some things I've had to do for the clan," Reive added, and Heikon felt a twinge of guilt. "I mean, given the choice between fixing toilets or going out as one of the clan enforcers ..." He hesitated and looked off at nothing, rather than at the phone resting on his knees. "If the clan needs me, I'll do it. But ... this is nice. A quiet life, where the worst things I have to worry about are cleaning up little-kid messes and taking apart toilets."

There was really nothing Heikon could think to say to that. He thought, once again, of Reive as Heikon had last seen him before twenty years of exile: a bright-eyed, laughing teenager, who had gloried in shifting into his copper-and-red dragon.

Twenty years of living under Braun's rule of terror in the mountain had turned him into this quiet, brooding young man. It would have been worse for Reive than for many others in the mountain, because Braun, the ringleader of the conspiracy against Heikon, was Reive's grandfather, and his father had also been among the conspirators. Against them, Reive had had no choice. They had taken him, trained him, taught him to kill.

Reive had been one of the first allies Heikon had gained in the mountain when he'd come back from exile. *"Please,"* Reive had said—begged, almost. *"I'm on your side. I want to help you—"*

"Take them down."

They were deep in the bowels of the tunnels beneath the mountains. Heikon knew these tunnels better than anyone else; he had dug them, or had them dug. No one else now living remembered all the ways in and out of the mountain, not even Braun, which meant that no one could keep him out, even if his brother ruled the clan with claws of iron.

Still, he had expected that sooner or later he would meet guards. He didn't want to hurt anyone, if he could help it. If they were outsiders he would have killed them without mercy, but these were his own people, his own family. He believed that only a few of them were on Braun's side. Somehow he had to sort out the traitors from the rest.

He didn't recognize Reive at first, this tall, strong young man in black, greatly changed from the boy Heikon remembered. But Reive remembered him.

In front of Heikon, Reive went to his knees and bowed his dark-haired head. He was dressed in black leathers for riding or fighting, but his hands were empty of weapons, resting loosely beside his knees on the tunnel's stone floor.

"I swear my allegiance to you," Reive said quietly. "I renounce my grandfather and father. If you don't believe me, kill me here and now."

"I believe you." Heikon took him by the arm and helped him up.

Reive refused to meet his eyes. "I've done terrible things, Uncle," he said quietly. "You don't want to know the things they've made me do."

"It doesn't matter now. All that matters is that you are sworn to me now, and I will take my mountain back."

Yes. Reive had been one of the first.

∼

But *I didn't repay your loyalty well, did I, nephew?* Heikon thought, looking at Reive's tired face on the phone's small screen. When he took back control of the mountain from his brother two years ago, he had been in need of trained enforcers that he could trust, particularly those who knew something about the world outside the mountain. Whenever he needed someone to go on a mission for him, to fight or spy, Reive had been one of the first he'd turned to. And Reive was good at it.

It had never occurred to him that Reive might crave a quiet life.

"What do you want, nephew?" he asked gently.

Reive gave a soft laugh, rolling his head against the wall. "You know, right now, I think it's just this. Taking care of the kids. Living in the mountain. Taking apart toilets. Oh, sure, I'd love to find my mate, but I've got hundreds of years to do that." He tilted his head, looking down at the phone screen again, his dark eyes serious. "You brought peace to us, Uncle. With my grandfather and father dead, there won't be any more fighting, and we can finally restore the mountain to what it was meant to be."

"Yes," Heikon said quietly. "Good night, Reive."

"Good night, Uncle."

Heikon broke the connection and held the phone for a moment, curled loosely in his hand.

With my grandfather and father dead ...

If only, Heikon thought. If only.

That was certainly what he *wanted* people to think. It was the story he'd put around, that he'd executed everyone directly involved with the conspiracy, and extracted oaths of loyalty from the rest.

In truth, most of the conspirators had renounced Braun

and gone back over to Heikon's side as soon as he came back. Some of them had died in the fighting, including Reive's father. And as for Braun ...

Well. He wouldn't be hurting anyone anymore.

Still ... with Esme back in his life, Heikon thought, maybe it was best to make sure that his precautions were holding. He dialed another number, one that he didn't call nearly as often as he should.

She might not be awake, he reminded himself. But then, she didn't sleep much, as was often true of the old. And indeed, she picked up on the first ring.

"Hi, Mother," he said.

"Sweetheart." Her voice was warm, though a little shaky with age.

Dragons lived a long time, but still, his mother was the oldest dragon he'd ever personally known. It was she who had brought the cherry-tree seeds that had grown into his heart-grove, long ago when she had swum across the sea from her native Japan, to a rugged, wild coastline of trees and mountains.

He had asked her, once, why she'd done it. *Because I wanted to see what was on the other side of the sea,* she'd said.

But she didn't travel anymore. She had a sanctuary of her own, deep in the mountains, and there she preferred to stay, these days, tending the gardens she loved ... and keeping his other secret.

"How's my brother?" he asked.

"Tranked into a coma as usual," his mother said dryly. "I'm not going to let him come out of it enough to escape, Heikon. I know what he's like—what he *is*."

Do you? Heikon wondered. Leaving Braun with his mother was the only solution he'd been able to think of, short of outright killing him. And when it came right down to it, he had been a little surprised to find that he didn't have it in him to kill his brother in cold blood.

"I hope not," he said. "He *mustn't* escape, Mother. I ..." He lowered his voice, though he knew Esme couldn't possibly be near enough to hear; in the quiet of the empty building, he would have heard her approach. "I found Esme again."

"That pretty little girl from the Lavigna clan? How nice for you, dear."

"She ..." He started to say it. And then he choked on the words. *She's my mate.* But it wasn't true anymore, and telling his mother now would force him to explain why he hadn't told her all those years ago. It had been so new, so fresh, a secret just for the two of them ... and then gone, in a single beat of his poisoned heart.

"She's just like I remember," he said instead. "Beautiful. Fiery."

"She always was an energetic girl," his mother mused. "They're the best kind, you know."

"I know," he said, smiling despite himself as he thought of Esme's temper.

"Just don't get too attached. Remember, there's a mate out there for you somewhere."

His chest gave a deep pang. "I know, Mother."

"And bring my grandchildren to visit one of these days!"

To a cave with Braun in it? Still ... he was locked up and drugged. Heikon knew he was going to have to get over it sooner or later, going to have to either trust that his mother could keep the rest of the clan safe from Braun—or go ahead and commit the act of fratricide he'd been trying to avoid.

It was easier for humans. *They* had police and courts and jails. Dragons resolved disputes themselves, frequently through duels. Usually it was simpler. But sometimes you ran into situations like this, when you had someone who was too dangerous to run around, but no safe place to put them.

"Heikon? Are you still there? Has this phone lost you?"

"No, no, I'm still here, Mother. I'll bring them someday soon. I have to go. I love you."

He put the phone away and got up decisively. After washing his hands thoroughly, he donned his jacket and looked around to be sure the bathroom was as tidy as he could leave it. He had no idea where Esme had gotten the tools from, so he'd left them packed up and ready for her to put them away.

He hoped she was happy with this gift. Tomorrow he would find more gifts to bring her. And maybe someday, she would take him back.

Just don't get too attached. His mother's words rang in his ears. *Remember, there's a mate out there for you somewhere.*

Wise words. But wrong.

There was no one for him but Esme. Not now. Not ever.

He left, turning off the lights as he went. At the door, he punched in the alarm code. It appeared to be a date, and he'd already finished typing it in and slipped through the door before the significance of it hit him.

It was the date they'd met. The day they had looked into each other's eyes and seen their forever love, their partner, their fated mate looking back at them.

With the ludicrous frog umbrella dangling from one hand, rain falling lightly on his hair and shoulders, he turned and looked up at Esme's building.

All the lights were off except several on the top floor. She had big windows that must offer a commanding view of the area, though nothing like the view from his mountain, of course.

As he watched, a slim shadow crossed one of the windows. Esme, going about her nighttime business. The shadow paused. Was she looking out now, or looking away, consumed with her own thoughts? What might she be doing up there?

He saw her, in his mind, as clearly as if she was in front of him, the way he remembered her at the Aerie twenty years ago. Wrapped in a silken green robe, a cup of tea in her hands, her hair spilling loose and long over her shoulders ...

Up there. Out of reach. And forever to remain so, if he couldn't find a way to win back her love.

He turned away before he could do something foolish, like calling her. She had extended a gesture of trust to him with the alarm code, and her willingness to leave him alone in her building; he was not oblivious to how much that meant to a dragon. So he must return her gesture of trust, and show her that he could be trusted not to push too far.

Patience, he thought. He had been apart from her for twenty years. Another night would not kill him. All good things in life were worth doing properly. He would win her back, and he would do it according to the rules she'd set him.

He was starting to come alive, feeling eagerness quickening inside him. She hadn't sent him away out of hand, when she easily could have. There *was* something between them still. He wasn't the only one who felt it.

Behind one of the buildings, hidden from casual observers by the night and the lightly falling rain, he shifted and stretched his wings, and took to the sky.

ESME

Rain was still falling the next day, steady and gray, as if to match Esme's mood. It had not helped when she came downstairs and found the toilet fixed, the tools neatly packed up and set to the side.

She knew how late he'd been there because she had been watching out the window, looking down on the rain-washed street ... waiting for him to leave. She had watched Heikon looking up at her apartment, and wondered if he sensed her looking down at him. She didn't want to stand there and watch him leave, but she couldn't help herself. She watched until he was out of sight, and then stood gazing a little while longer until she forced herself to turn back to the suddenly empty-feeling apartment.

She did *not* miss him. It was absurd. And yet, it seemed as if having him come back into her life had made her aware of a hole that had been there all along, a hole shaped exactly like Heikon, that only he could fill.

It was foolish. It was *stupid*. For one thing, he was no longer her mate. The bond had been well and truly broken. She could not possibly still miss him this much; she had grieved him for years and then gotten past it and moved on with her life.

And now here he was again, and it felt as if she had stepped directly back into a wellspring of feelings she'd thought long dead and buried.

Humans fall in love and get married without a mate bond all the time. Is it truly so foolish to think ...

Yes. Yes, it was. For one thing, she was *not* a human. And she'd had lovers before. One of those liaisons had given her Melody, who she wouldn't trade for the world.

There had been genuine emotion between Esme and all of her previous lovers. But at the same time, it had been a shallow sort of thing, never able to deepen into the true life-long connection she craved. She'd always been aware of her dragon inside her, pushing her away, urging her to wait for her true mate. When she had looked into Heikon's eyes and recognized their bond, her dragon had risen in joy. It was as if she'd been filled with pure music, from the bottom of her soul to the ends of her fingertips. It was the thing she had waited for her whole life.

And now it was back to being one of those shallow, empty relationships that could never deepen further. Having her dragon react to Heikon the way that it had to her previous lovers—with a constant thrumming refrain of *This is not our mate*—hurt her in a deep kind of way that she could hardly bear. If she acted cold around him, it was only because she could not bear to look into his face and hear her dragon sulkily insist they were wasting time with this man who was not their mate, rather than feeling it leap with joy as it strained to reaffirm the bond of their shared souls.

How could you share that kind of connection with someone and then go back to being near-strangers?

Somehow Heikon seemed to be managing just fine, she

thought bitterly, as she picked up the toolbox and took it back to its closet.

～

"Where's that handsome boy?" Miriam quavered when her granddaughter dropped her off for class, half an hour early as usual. Miriam always liked some time to get settled in before the other students arrived.

"I'm quite sure I don't know or care. Can I help you with your shawl?"

Miriam was bundled as if to face an Arctic expedition rather than a late summer rainstorm. Getting old must be a terrible thing for humans, Esme thought, helping her peel off her damp outer shawl only to reveal another shawl underneath, wrapped around her bony shoulders.

And Miriam was so young, why, she was barely 90! Esme tried to recall what she had been doing when she turned 90. Hmm, possibly she'd been living in New York at that time. Jazz had just become a thing, and there was a lot of interesting music to collect. Those early years of records had been such a wonderful thing. Esme had never dreamed in her childhood that she would someday be able to hoard music in physical objects she could possess, rather than just in the form of sheet music and instruments and the contents of her own head.

"Oh, there he is," Miriam said with satisfaction in her birdlike voice, and Esme looked up, startled. Heikon was just coming in the door, shaking rain off that utterly ridiculous frog umbrella. Today he wore a jacket of deep amethyst, setting off his bronze skin and sparking purple glints from his dark eyes.

She had found his red jacket slightly inappropriate and

ridiculous yesterday, but she now realized it was only that it was a little out of place in an old-fashioned way that she couldn't help finding incredibly charming today. Men simply didn't dress like that anymore. Even George, who thought he was dapper, wore his pants halfway up to his armpits, and his beige jackets never went out of fashion mainly because they hadn't been in fashion to begin with.

But Heikon had grown up in an era when male fashion was as much of an art as the female sort, and it seemed he'd never quite lost the knack. He walked in like a man who knew he looked good and expected all eyes to turn to him— as of course they did—but *his* gaze went straight to Esme, and she was shocked and alarmed to feel herself blushing, especially when he broke into a welcoming smile. Esme had to fight to straighten out her own lips.

Ever the gracious hostess, she went to welcome him, despite her overwhelming desire to find something urgent to fuss with at the coffee table, or possibly hide in a closet until everyone left.

"Esmerelda," he murmured as she reached to take his umbrella. "You look lovely tonight."

So do you. She caught herself right before she blurted it out aloud. He *did*, though, damn it. Lovely wasn't quite the right word, but ... *dashing. Handsome. Cheekbones you could cut yourself on.* She'd forgotten what his eyes were like, dark and deep, eyes you could get lost in ...

She spun away from him hastily, before her treacherous arms could reach for him, seeking the touch of his skin again. "You'll be dancing with Miriam tonight," she said shortly. "You're the only two here yet, so you'll have a bit of time to get acquainted. Let me go put some music on."

She took her time fussing with the record player and sound system, but she couldn't help watching out of the corner of her eye. Heikon, to her surprise, went to one knee in front of Miriam's fragile, hunched figure in the wheelchair, as courtly as a prince in a queen's kingdom. "Care to dance with me tonight, lady?" he asked, holding out a hand. His deep voice carried across the room, brought to Esme by the perfect acoustics that she'd spent so much time carefully planning into the ballroom's design.

Miriam laughed quietly and put out her thin hands. "I would love to, but don't let me keep you away from that beautiful redhead all evening."

Esme put the record needle down and cranked up the sound, drowning out whatever he might have replied in the clear strains of Chopin.

~

She had already decided she was not going to dance with Heikon tonight. Too much temptation lay that way. So she paired him up first with one of her students, then another.

If you truly wanted to remove temptation, all you have to do is send him away ...

Instead she watched with a critical eye as he danced with first one old lady, then another. She started out fully prepared to stop the dance if he was in any way rude to her students, but she might have known he'd be perfectly polite, endlessly patient. And Esme was amused to see that most of her students knew more about dancing than Heikon did. They had, after all, been coming to her classes for weeks. It wasn't that Heikon couldn't dance, just that his was a beginner's understanding of the steps, or perhaps that of a man who hadn't done it in, perhaps, a century or more.

But he was graceful and coordinated, far more so than many people she'd taught. Perhaps more to the point, he was surprisingly gracious and humble about letting the other

67

students—elderly human women, no less—show him the dance steps and correct the ones he missed.

It was always a pleasure seeing her students become teachers. Esme liked to pair up inexperienced students with the class veterans, because she knew that they would both get something out of the experience; the newcomers would learn the steps, of course, but teaching someone else was a good way to get the experienced students out of their rut and give them a new perspective. You learned a lot from showing someone else how to do something.

And tonight, it was even more pleasing to watch them than usual, because Heikon was such a good student. She would never have thought it possible, and yet, he was. He accepted correction with only a slight, chagrined smile, and he brought out the best in his dance partners, as only a dancing natural could.

Dancing was inherently a generous act. Selfish people might do well in solo dance, but Esme had a private theory that they could not dance well with a partner. Coupled dancing meant giving part of yourself to your partner. It meant being willing to let the other person shine rather than trying to take the glory for yourself. For it was only when you gave yourself completely to your partner, when you elevated their glory above your own, that the two of you could become greater together than you would ever be apart.

Watching Heikon dance with the other women in the class—watching him bring out the best in each of them, watching him make these old women smile, make them laugh ... she was wildly, stupidly jealous. She had thought it would get easier once her treacherous heart recognized that it was simply the meaningless steps of a dance ... but instead it got worse.

She knew it was ridiculous. *She* was ridiculous! It had been her idea in the first place.

It was just that *she* wanted to be out there on his arm. *She* wanted Heikon to whirl her around the dance floor, lifting her as though she was weightless.

The only person stopping you is you, she told herself.

I don't know why you're so interested in him anyway, her dragon remarked.

... and there was the reminder of why she couldn't. Because she never could be with him the way she wanted. Oh, they could be lovers; in time, she might even love him. But there would always be that deepest part of her soul holding back.

How could you do this to us? she thought, heart breaking, as she watched him whirl around the dance floor, with a succession of different women in his arms where she desperately wanted to be. *I know you broke the mate bond because you thought it would protect me. But once it's gone, it's gone. We can't get it back, and now we will always have our animals pushing us apart.*

I don't know how you think it's possible to go back to how we used to be.

With a deep sigh, she went to dance with George again. It was like dancing with a block of wood, compared to Heikon.

And yet, the evening passed in a whirl of music and dance, as it always did on dance-class nights. Despite Esme's private unhappiness, she still managed to lose herself in the music to the point that it seemed all too soon when her students began to gather their coats and umbrellas, and Miriam's granddaughter came to take her back to the care home.

And then, after the flurry of goodbyes and see-you-

Thursdays, it was just her and Heikon, as he helped her clean up the coffee things, helpful and uncomplaining.

"Any more toilets for me to fix?" he asked, with a sparkle of humor in his eye.

Esme hmmph'd and firmly resisted the urge to go off and secretly flush a shoe down the toilet. There had been something indescribably ... well ... *hot* about Heikon down on the floor, jacket off and shirt sleeves rolled up.

She liked him well put together, in his nice suits with his hair tucked into place. But she liked him even more with his clothes off, all sweaty, doing things with his hands ...

Okay, this was going to *entirely* the wrong mental place.

She realized she'd missed all of what he'd just said. "I'm sorry, what?"

Heikon smiled patiently and said, "I was just going to get something to eat. I'm hungry. Would you like to join me?"

Temptation drew her with the strength of an undertow. But going out to eat felt like a date. *Far* too much like a date. "I prefer to eat in," she said, which wasn't precisely true—but now that she thought about it, had been increasingly true lately. She really *was* turning into a recluse.

And then her traitorous mouth opened and said something completely absurd: "But you can join me tonight if you like."

What. What. WHAT.

Heikon stared at her. If he'd said anything smug in that moment, she would have taken back her offer so fast it'd make his head spin. But instead, a look of startled warmth spread across his face, his eyes softening in a way that sent shivers straight down to her core.

"I'd love to," he said, in a voice as warm and gentle as his eyes.

Esme hastily turned away and began making little adjustments to the coffee cups that were already clean and dry and put away.

A whole evening with Heikon in her apartment! What was she thinking!

Yes, her dragon said, *what were you thinking? What if our mate shows up and HE'S there?*

A freshly horrifying thought occurred to her. What if her dragon was right? What if, now that the mate bond with Heikon was broken, she *did* have a mate out there somewhere? What if she fell in love with Heikon, and then met her *real* mate—

"Are you all right?" Heikon asked. Esme turned; he was holding out a hand partway, as if he wanted to touch her but had stopped himself. He took a breath and she could see him visibly gathering himself. "If you don't want to, it's all right. Really. It is."

And *that* was what made her put her mental foot down, right through her dragon's objections. He was being so *careful* with her. She had always thought of Heikon as forceful and arrogant—and he was, when it counted. But he was handling her with the most delicate touch. He had to be working so hard on it. Fighting was easy for dragons. To be gentle, to be kind, to hold onto something precious so carefully that it could escape if it needed to—those were the hard things.

She ... she didn't *want* to send him away.

"One condition," she said.

"Anything."

"I'm not picking up anything special for you. Dinner is going to be made out of whatever's in my fridge, and no complaining."

"Never," he said earnestly.

How was it that he could disarm her with the simplest statements? She turned away before she could give in to the urges consuming her—to reach out, to take his hand, to fall into his arms ...

As she took the lead to the stairwell, she wondered how she was going to get through this evening without doing any of those things. And she wondered, also, whether she really wanted to.

HEIKON

J ust inside the door of her apartment, Esme stopped
and slipped off her shoes. Heikon followed suit,
although he wasn't sure if it was one of her family
customs or if she simply wanted to get out of her
high-heeled dancing shoes.

Taking off his shoes made him feel oddly vulnerable. He
wiggled his toes in his dark socks and then followed Esme
into the kitchen, looking around curiously all the while.

Her apartment was built on an open plan, emphasizing its
size and space and high ceilings. Up here the building's
origins as a warehouse were more obvious than downstairs,
where paneling and interior walls made it look like any ordinary convention space. In the penthouse, Esme had left the
brick and woodwork exposed, giving it a raw and unfinished
look, slightly old-fashioned and yet trendy, that Heikon
found pleasing.

The juxtaposition of antique and modern, relaxed and
upscale, continued throughout the rest of the apartment. She
had a full-sized grand piano near comfortable-looking
squashy couches and chairs, a state-of-the-art entertainment

system with a giant, expensive-looking wall-mounted flatscreen next to colorful, framed folk art.

It was an interesting apartment. Some places had their owners' personalities stamped on them, and this was one of those places. Everywhere he looked, Heikon saw Esme. It made him wonder, for the first time, what aspects of him other people saw in his mountain.

"Wine?" Esme asked, rummaging in cabinets in the big open kitchen. "Coffee? Tea?"

"Wine would be appreciated. Thank you."

She poured a glass, and handed it to him. Her fingers did not quite brush his, but the glass seemed a little warmer where she had touched it.

The kitchen was like the rest of the apartment, spacious and tastefully appointed. Heikon started to sit at the granite-topped kitchen island, then went to the window instead.

It was not, of course, as fine a view as the view from the top of his mountain. Not at all. But she did have a good view of the surrounding streets, spread out around her penthouse. From their vantage here, only four stories above the ground, it was possible to see all the details that would have been hidden from higher up. He watched a pair of humans come out of one of the shops, carrying bags and chattering to each other.

It was like the difference between flying over a forest very high, with the trees all blurring together into a green carpet far below, and soaring at treetop level, able to see each deer that sprang away, each small brook twisting between its mossy banks. From a great distance, the world became an abstract of shapes and colors—like the forests and valleys at the base of his mountain, spread out like a patchwork quilt. But up close, viewed from above, you could start to see how it all went together. You began to recognize the patterns of life there, the habits of its creatures, the changing ways of the seasons.

It was like gardening, in a way. From far away, the gardens were beautiful, but only as a tapestry of colors that might as well be a photograph. It was only up close, with your hands in the dirt, that you could begin to understand and appreciate them.

These streets, he realized, were Esme's garden.

"Something fascinating down there?" Esme asked. She leaned past him to look down at the streets glistening in the rain.

"Just ..." *Seeing you. Maybe for the first time.*

When he didn't finish the thought, she turned to look at him. Her eyes were very large and green, her face very close to his. There was a faint blush on her lips from the wine.

And then she jerked back. "Dinner," she said, as if reminding herself. "It's not going to be much. Just pasta and a salad."

"Can I help at all?"

"Sure." She took a lettuce and placed it in his hands. "You can make the salad."

They worked side by side in the kitchen, chopping ingredients. Just pasta, she'd said, but he could tell as she browned onions with an expert hand that it would be good.

"Do you like to cook?" he asked her. It was slowly dawning on him how little he knew about her. They had come together in a rush at the Aerie for a brief and wonderful affair, but now he began to realize how little they'd gotten to know each other as people. Her hobbies, her interests, her likes and dislikes were still largely a closed book to him.

"I have Italian blood. Of course I do." She smiled. "No, in seriousness, the urge comes and goes. When I first move to any new city, usually I relish the novelty of having new restaurants to explore. But a few years into it, I find myself cooking at home more often. I enjoy the comfort of it. The homeyness, you might say." She turned to scoop up a handful of the tomatoes and red peppers he was chopping. "And, of course, it *was* the way I grew up. Back in the old country, we had a private hunting preserve in the Alps, and Dad always insisted that we learn to cook everything we killed."

She stirred the sizzling contents of the skillet and reached up with the back of her hand to push her hair out of her eyes. It was still pinned up for dancing, but some strands had begun to work their way loose, straggling down on her forehead in the heat from the stove.

"What about you?" she asked. "I'm sure you had people to cook for you, back in the mountain."

He had been so captivated by listening to her talk about herself—her every word, her every move—that he had to forcibly reroute himself to thinking about his own life. "It's more of a group effort. We have a rotating cooking roster, and yes, I take turns too."

"Heikon Corcoran, cooking for a crowd." She laughed, and it took his breath away. He had almost forgotten how beautiful her laugh was. "Now I'm picturing you peeling potatoes, like in those cartoons of humans being punished that way."

"I can't see what would be a punishment about it. It's peaceful—or it would be, at least, if the kids weren't flying in and out all the time, trying to grab a snack."

She laughed that delightful laugh again. "Our family get-togethers were always much more sedate. But then, we're a very small clan."

"You're from Switzerland, right?" He located her dishes in an antique-looking glass-fronted cabinet, and took down two plates.

"We're Italian-Swiss, yes. We have some little chalets up in the mountains. A separate home for each family. For the most part, when I was a child, it was just me and my parents, as well as a few staff. Of course, my cousins and aunts and uncles would visit. It was only a short flight." She smiled wistfully. "I envied you, with your big family in that mountain."

Heikon laughed. "Meanwhile, I sought out solitude in my gardens whenever I could. It can be a little bit noisy and crowded in there. Or at least I used to. All those years of—"

He stopped. He didn't like to think about those years, his exile years. He had spent part of that time living in caves in the mountains, healing and recovering, barely aware of the human part of himself. At first life had only been about surviving. Then it had been focused on revenge. His entire life had revolved around taking back what was his, reclaiming the *life* that was his.

"I think the pasta's almost done," Esme said, breaking the silence. Her voice was formal, and the easy camaraderie they'd fallen into had once again strained.

Because she'd gone through her own kind of hell in those years, hadn't she? Believing him dead, trying to move on with her life ...

Losing your mate was the worst thing that could happen to a shifter. Many didn't survive it. That Esme had not only survived, but thrived, made him aware of how incredibly strong she was.

They had both survived. And now here they were, twenty years later, picking up the pieces.

He laid out the plates, and Esme dished up pasta with a simple pan-seared mix of onions, peppers, and tomatoes. With some freshly grated parmesan and the salad on the side, it was simple and yet excellent. It occurred to Heikon that he'd had very few meals in his life that did not involve meat in one form or another, and before he could stop himself he'd already said so.

"I believe in exploring my options," Esme said. "The humans have such a vast array of recipes that don't involve meat at all. And the Internet is an excellent source of instruction. I've taken to watching cooking shows on Netflix to relax."

Heikon, who had not known that cooking shows were a thing that existed, merely nodded as he twirled spaghetti around his fork.

All in all, this was not the lonely, empty existence he'd expected. Her apartment was warm and nice and full of things she clearly loved. She didn't even seem unhappy.

Was there even still a place for him in her life?

But then he looked across the table at her, and caught the shadow of sorrow in her eyes before she dropped her gaze to her plate. He could no longer see her animal in her eyes, but he could still read her emotions as if they were his own. And her pain still hurt him.

"Show me," he said, unable to think of anything else to say.

She gave him a sharp, startled look. "Show you what?"

"This Netflix of yours. It's important to you. I'd like to see it and share it, if I might."

"I—It's not—Well, all right."

She reached for a slim black object on the edge of the table and pointed it at the flatscreen. Heikon jumped only slightly when the screen lit up. Oh right, remote controls. The mountain had a lot of this newfangled technology now because the younger members of the clan wanted it, and he had to admit that it was handy. But he didn't often use it just for fun.

Esme flicked through different options on the TV and soon there was a show with humans doing things with pie crusts and fillings. In truth, he was bored within a few minutes (his dragon was idly clicking its claws and muttering things about hunting), but what fascinated him was her obvious fascination. It wasn't quite as intense as when she focused on music, but he loved seeing that sharp interest and attention on her face.

"You really love this kind of thing, don't you?" Heikon said. "Cooking shows. Dancing classes. All of it."

"Well, it's my life, Heikon." Her eyes sparkled suddenly, a playful flare he hadn't seen in a very long time. "Don't you love your mountain? Your gardens?"

"Of course. I was thinking earlier ..." But then he hesitated, not sure if he wanted to share his mental comparison between the neighborhood and his own gardens; he didn't know how she'd take it. "It's not different," he finished weakly.

Esme laughed. "Of course not."

She got up and reached for the salad bowl. Heikon helped her put the dishes in the sink.

"We can do them later," she said, wiping her hands on a dish towel. "It's ... nice, having company up here. I don't often have guests, except when Melody and her mate are here."

That's right. He'd last seen Melody when she was a little girl. "How is your daughter? She's found her mate?"

"Yes, she has." Esme's eyes sparkled, her whole face becoming animated; her obvious love for her daughter shone through. "I have to say that I wasn't sure what to think when I first met him. He's an ex-con, more tattoos than you care to mention ... I just hoped he'd be good to my little girl. But he is. You should see them together. Oh here, let me show you a picture."

She pulled one down off the wall. The dark-haired woman in the photo was almost unrecognizable as that skinny girl Heikon had seen at the mountain all those years ago. A blond man in the photo had his arms around her.

"They look like a wonderful couple," Heikon said.

"They are. She's pregnant, can you believe it? I'm going to be a grandmother." She laughed softly. "I'm sure that's no big deal for you. You've had a long time to adjust to the idea. You have great-grandkids, don't you?" He nodded. "But it's new for me. It makes me feel old."

"Trust me, Esme," he said gently. "You're anything but old."

He reached out, prepared to withdraw if she said anything, did anything, to suggest she didn't want—but instead she leaned forward, and when the side of his hand brushed her face, she leaned into it like a cat leaning into a friendly caress.

It was only another step to close the distance between them, and then his lips touched hers for the first time in twenty years.

The mate bond might be gone, but her lips hadn't changed at all. There was no longer the fire lighting up the channel between them—instead it felt like coming home, like finding a place he'd lost long ago.

There was a vanilla-flavored sweetness on her lips, and she opened her mouth, inviting him in. The sensation of her mouth on his was like a rush of heat and honey, filling him from his toes to the top of his head. Dimly he was aware that he had one hand in her hair, the other on her hip, and her arms were around him, and he was home, home, *home*—

And then she pulled away.

The kiss broke. She took a step backward. He resisted for a bare instant, everything in him crying out against the loss of that homecoming feeling, and then he let her go and she took a few quick steps away, putting some distance between them again.

"Esme," he said. He was still breathless from that kiss, that *kiss.* "You can't tell me you didn't feel anything just then."

"It wasn't what we had before." She sounded like she was trying to convince herself as much as him.

"So we'll make something new."

"Heikon ....." She reached for the dish towel and worked it anxiously between her hands. "Why did you *do* it?"

"Why did I—what?"

"The mate bond." She was looking everywhere except at him, plucking at the dish towel, twisting it, wringing it. "Once it's gone, it's gone. How could you do that to us?"

And then it hit him, all in a shocking rush. *She thought he'd done it on purpose.*

"Esme," he said, stunned.

All these years, she thought he did it on *purpose*?

No wonder she was so furious with him. He now admired her self-restraint for not simply punching him in the face the first time she saw him at the Aerie.

She turned away abruptly. "Never mind. I don't know why I thought ..."

"Esme. No. Wait, listen—" He held out a hand, but all her body language said *Don't touch*, and all he did was brush it lightly through the air above her shoulder. As if she'd felt it anyway, she turned her head. "Esme, it wasn't *me*. It was my brother."

He could have laughed, and stopped himself only because he knew how it would sound to her. He felt giddy with excitement. If *that* was all that was keeping them apart, then just telling her the truth would fix it.

Could it really be that simple?

Esme turned to look at him full on, her green eyes dark with suspicion. "Heikon ..."

"It was Braun, Esme. He poisoned me with concentrated dragonsbane. I survived only because I managed to get away before I took a lethal dose." But close enough. It all rushed back to him: the pain, the disorientation, and most of all the feeling of Esme suddenly vanishing, as if the bond had been cut with a knife. "Braun thought I was dead."

"We all thought you were dead," Esme said. Puzzlingly, she didn't look like she was softening a bit. In fact, she looked even more angry now.

"I know, and I'm so sorry for that. I had to let people think so while Braun was in charge of the Aerie. The only person I dared trust with it was Mother—"

"You told your *mother* and not me?"

"I had to keep you safe!"

"I *know* that!" Her voice came out like a whipcrack. "I thought you were dead, Heikon! All this time ... all this time, I thought you were dead, and then I found out you were alive and you didn't even trust me enough to tell me."

"But ..." He couldn't understand why this wasn't working. "I didn't *want* to sever the bond, don't you see? It wasn't me!"

"I never thought you *wanted* to sever it, Heikon! Aaaaah!" With a cry of frustration, she hurled the wadded-up towel, now twisted nearly into a knot, to land in the sink. "I *know* you didn't want to break it! But whether you did it on purpose to protect me, or just went with it, what it comes down to is that you let me spend twenty years thinking you were dead. You could have come to me. We could have dealt with Braun together. But no, you had to handle it all on your own! And *then*!"

She seemed to be working herself up to increased heights of frustration and anger. Words spilled out of her—words he sensed she'd been holding inside for a long time.

"You say you were trying to protect me, but what were you protecting me from when you'd deposed your brother and you didn't even bother to tell me you were alive then? I had to hear about it through the dragon grapevine, Heikon! I found out from *Darius*! Tell me again who you were trying to protect. Was it me, or yourself?"

All he could do was stare at her. He'd never really thought about it that way before. He'd thought of himself as the victim of Braun's treachery, and Esme as a potential second victim, who had to be kept safe from all of that.

I couldn't come to you because—

Because ... why? To keep her safe? Or because he couldn't face her without the mate bond, knowing all that they'd lost?

"I didn't know *how*," he said helplessly. "I really did want to keep you safe, Esme. But ... you're right. I didn't know what I could say that would make up for what had happened."

"Oh, Heikon." She buried her face in her hands and turned away.

This was all going wrong. He could feel her slipping away from him. Rather than the grand reunion he'd envisioned, now the distance between them was growing by the moment.

You'll find others, his dragon said placatingly. *Our mate is out there for us. She'll be everything we've always dreamed of—*

"Shut up!"

"What?" Esme said, turning to stare at him with wide eyes —still dry, but looking like tears might not be far away.

"Not you!" Heikon said, horrified. "I was talking to my dragon."

"Oh." She almost smiled. "Yes, my dragon's having a word or two about this now, too. I think you can guess what she's saying."

"Yes," he said.

There were only a few feet between them, but it might as well be a thousand miles. And for the first time in his life, Heikon didn't *care* what his dragon thought. Having her so close, yet separated from him by walls of hurt and suspicion, tore his heart in half.

"Is there any way I can make up for it?" he asked. "Is there any way we can get back what we had?"

"We can't! It's gone, Heikon. I don't know why I thought it was worth trying again." She blinked her eyes vigorously.

Heikon desperately wanted to take her into his arms, to soothe that devastated look away—but how could he help when he was the cause of it?

"Do you think it's truly gone, Esme? Because I don't. Look into your heart. Ask your heart what it wants."

She gave a sort of a smile, more like a grimace, and dashed at her eyes. "Ask my heart? I keep asking my heart, Heikon. I've done nothing but ask my heart. My dragon *is* my heart, and every time I ask, I get the same answer. And I think you do too."

Not our mate, his dragon said, and Heikon echoed it soundlessly, his lips shaping the words.

"Now leave, if you don't mind," Esme said quietly. "I'm going to cry and I don't want to do it in front of you."

"Esme—"

Anger flared again. "Go! And don't bother coming to the next dance session. I don't want you there, now or ever. It's going to be kinder on us both if we just stop pretending this can ever happen and move on with our lives."

"There is no life for me without you."

"*Stop* it!" Green flashed in her eyes, the suggestion of an oncoming transformation. "Don't you understand, Heikon? You're only hurting us both with this asinine insistence that we can go back to being the people we were twenty years ago. But we're *not* those people. Our decisions have changed us. Pretending otherwise will only break both our hearts."

"Isn't your heart breaking now, Esme?" His voice cracked as he said it.

"Of course it is!" she cried, flinging her hands out. "But at least it's breaking only once, rather than over and over again, for a lifetime, every time I'm reminded of what we used to be and what we no longer are. Go, Heikon, *please*!"

It was the *please* that did it. He could no more refuse a request from his mate than he could turn into a fish and swim away. He still paused with his hand on the door and looked back at her, over his shoulder.

Her hair was coming undone, falling over her shoulder in great swatches. Tears stood in her eyes. She was distraught and wild and still the most beautiful thing he'd ever seen.

"Don't give up on us, Esme. A clanlord does not beg, but I'm begging you."

"Go!" she said, and it was only as the door closed that he glimpsed her putting her face in her hands. That was his last sight of her, as she began to cry.

He stood for a long while outside her door. He couldn't bear to let go and give in, but what could he do when his mate herself refused to fight for what he knew was still between them?

At length, he went down the stairs, used the alarm code, and let himself out.

It wasn't over. He wouldn't *let* it be over. But it was clear that what they were doing now didn't seem to be working.

There is another way. I'll find it.

As he shifted and took to the skies, he thought, *I won't give up on us, Esme. Not now. Not ever.*

ESME

When she woke in the morning, alone in her too-large bed, Esme thought, *Today is the first day of the rest of my life.*

She kept thinking it, with great determination, as she went through her morning routine. She made herself a cup of tea and an omelet, and took both of them out to the rooftop deck, where she had patio furniture and a covered pavilion. It had finally stopped raining, but the weather was cool, and she wrapped a robe around her shoulders and looked across the rain-washed rooftop with its plastic chairs.

Today is the first day of the rest of my life. A nice happy life. Right? she asked her dragon.

Y...esss? her dragon replied.

That was not the solid affirmation she was hoping for.

Ever since last night—ever since she'd kissed Heikon—her dragon had been strangely distant. Its usual bold protests about Heikon not being their mate were muted. She would've thought it would be delighted to have Heikon out of their lives, even if she was still fighting with the prickling of tears whenever she thought about it. At the very least she would have thought she'd have her dragon's backing to put steel in her spine.

And now this.

He's not our mate, is he? she thought at her dragon, trying to suppress a quiver of hope. Maybe the kiss had brought it back. Maybe ...

No, her dragon returned. That, at least, was quick and sure. It had no doubts.

So what's bothering you?

I don't know, her dragon said. *Something's not right. None of this feels right. I just don't know why.*

It wasn't usually like this. For shifters, their inner beast was usually the most confident and sure part of them. It was their instinct, their deepest nature. It was the part that acted without thinking and needed to be reined in by the rational, human mind.

To have her animal expressing uncertainty and insecurity baffled her. Her dragon was the one with all the answers. Even when she disagreed with it, she relied on its rock-bottom certainty to give her strength.

And now, when she needed its stubborn self-assurance more than any other time in her life, it was going to do this?

You're very frustrating sometimes, you know that?

We could hunt, her dragon suggested, with an inward ruffle of wings.

Can't, she sighed. *I have responsibilities this afternoon.*

Inward sulking.

We'll fly later. I promise.

The idea of flying was enough to perk her up a bit. Still, she dragged through the morning and early afternoon, fighting periodic bouts of misery, hoping against hope that Heikon would walk through the door.

I did tell him to leave. In no uncertain terms.

Oh come on, he's not going to take that for an answer, is he?

Apparently he was.

~

A t least she was reasonably busy. She had an early-afternoon salsa class today, then the kiddie dance class she taught at 4 p.m. after school let out, and finally the regular ballroom class in the evening.

Usually one or another of her adult ballroom students came in to help with the kid class. Today it was Lupe. Esme thought at first that it was just her own dismal mood making it seem like something was bothering the human woman. Anyway, Lupe was always a little bit quiet and serious. But then Esme went back to the changing room to pick up a spare set of dance shoes for one of the kids, and heard weeping in the bathroom.

It's none of my business, she told herself. Whatever problems Lupe was having were probably human problems anyway, and not something she could understand or help with.

But still, after the class, when they were putting things away and preparing for the evening ballroom class, she noticed Lupe's eyes were red from weeping. Esme took a deep breath and decided to go for it. Maybe helping with a comparatively simple human problem would distract her from her own problems. "What's wrong?" she asked.

"It's only—it's George," Lupe cried, and burst into fresh tears.

Esme found herself in the awkward position of holding the shorter woman, patting her shoulder, while Lupe's tears dampened her dancing dress. "I ... er ... what is it? Is he ill?"

"No, he just ..." Lupe sniffled. "He doesn't even know I exist."

"That's hardly true," Esme said. She'd noticed who typically paired off in the class, and it seemed like George and Lupe danced together frequently.

"But he doesn't know how I feel about him." Lupe pulled away and wiped at her eyes. Esme gave her a handkerchief. "Thank you. I don't know what to do."

"Tell him?" Esme suggested. She honestly couldn't see what on earth Lupe saw in George, who to her seemed boring in the extreme. He was a former salesman who droned on constantly about every client he'd ever had. But everyone had different tastes, she supposed. There were probably those who would find Heikon insufferable and not to their tastes at all.

Surely not!

The thought came from her dragon.

I thought you didn't like him.

I don't not *like him,* her dragon said. *He's just not our mate, that's all. But he isn't boring!*

Meanwhile, the suggestion had triggered a fresh bout of weeping in Lupe, who was just getting herself under control enough to speak again. "What if he doesn't feel the same way? What if he laughs at me?"

"That's the risk you run, when you put your heart out there," Esme said. "But if you don't take chances, you'll never know, right?" She looked at Lupe, the small human woman living her short human life, and oddly determined to spend the rest of it (for reasons Esme couldn't fathom) with that dull salesman.

But he made Lupe happy. He made her laugh; his stories, trite as they seemed to Esme, could draw Lupe out of her shyness and make her come alive, sparkling in delight.

"You should listen to your heart," she said slowly, the words coming with increasing conviction from somewhere deep inside her. "A life in which you risk nothing is hardly a life worth living. If you don't ask, or if you ask and you're rejected, either way you'll have the same thing—nothing. But only one of those options gives you the chance of getting everything you wanted."

"I ... never thought about it that way," Lupe said damply, looking a little brighter.

"Neither did I," Esme said, almost to herself.

All throughout the evening class, her hopeful gaze kept slipping to the door. But it remained shut—stubbornly, cruelly shut. Wherever Heikon was, he wasn't here.

She had thought she wanted him to leave. She'd thought it would be better for both of them.

Now she kept thinking about her earlier advice to Lupe to take a chance, seize the moment.

It might be that there's another mate out there for each of us. It might be that we'd spend our lives unable to fully commit to each other, with our animals pushing us apart.

But ... what if I'm wrong?

The worst possible thing that could happen was that she'd end up alone, and that was what she had already.

She looked for Lupe and George, and found them dancing close together, with Lupe's head resting on his chest. Normally George rotated through all the female dance partners, but tonight he'd had eyes only for Lupe, and earlier this evening Esme had seen them over by the coffeepot with their heads together, talking quietly.

George and Lupe weren't the only ones who seemed happy tonight. Albert and Greta had been inseparable as usual, and tonight they had a new student, a tall gawky woman named Beatrice who had immediately gravitated toward Judy.

Esme wasn't sure if humans had mates in the same way shifters did, but there was no denying that there had been a connection between Judy and Beatrice as soon as their eyes met across the room. Right now Judy was showing Beatrice a sequence of dance steps, with her hand in the small of Beatrice's back, both their faces filled with animated delight.

All her students were pairing off, it seemed, while Esme danced alone.

"You seem sad, dear," Miriam said in her fragile voice when Esme came over to help her pour a cup of coffee. "Thank you."

"Only thinking about missed opportunities," Esme said. She leaned a hip against the table with the coffee things, and looked out at the dance floor. "Were you married, Miriam?"

Miriam smiled, and mischief danced in her eyes. "Three times."

"Really?" That was a lot, for humans. "Do you regret any of them?"

"Not a single moment. Well ..." She seemed to drift off into a wistful reverie. "Maybe Herbert. He did have a great love of the ponies. Gambling, you know," she added, seeing Esme's baffled look.

"Oh," Esme said. That did make a great deal more sense than horse shifters.

"But what that man could do after the lights went out ... oh yes," she said, sipping her coffee carefully with the cup held in both shaking hands. "No regrets."

"I'm glad for you," Esme said. Her heart ached.

"And what about you?" Miriam asked, looking up at her. "Where's your young man tonight?"

"My, er ... my what?" Esme was aware that her protest sounded extremely hollow.

"That lovely young man who's been coming in. Don't think I can't see the way you look at him. The entire class can see it." Miriam smiled. "Or didn't you notice that in a group of people rather over-burdened with single women, nobody set their cap for that stunningly handsome young man?"

"He was mobbed by every woman in the room the minute he walked in, Miriam," Esme said dryly. "Including you."

Miriam laughed, a bell-like sound that made her sound much younger. In times like that, Esme glimpsed the woman she'd been, a woman who must have turned heads everywhere she went (and three heads in particular, apparently). "Oh, you can't blame a girl for wanting a little attention from a man who looks like *that*. But no one stuck around—didn't you notice that? All he had to do was reach a hand for you, and everyone got out of the way. And you should have seen your face."

Esme touched her face as if it had suddenly changed on her. "What do you mean?"

"You light up when that man walks in the room, sweetheart," Miriam said gently. "All the time I've been coming to this class, you seemed a little bit sad. It was the first time I've ever seen you without that shadow in your eyes."

Surely not, she thought. There had still been a shadow across both of them, the shadow of what they'd once been and could never be again.

"Heikon and I have a history, Miriam," she said. "It's complicated and sad."

"Doesn't every great love affair have some tragedy in it?"

"We don't have a great love affair."

But we did, didn't we? she thought. For a few moments there, before things fell apart, it had felt like a love to shake the world. It had been the sort of love that humans wrote ballads about, singing them long after the lovers had vanished in dust.

"There," Miriam said. There was satisfaction in her

cracked voice. "That's the look, right there. You're thinking about him, aren't you?"

Esme started to protest, but what was the point? "Yes," she said, and for the first time all day, she could feel a genuine smile peeking out.

"And why are you here with us old biddies when you could be where he is?"

"Well, for one thing, because someone has to switch out the records," she said, noticing the music had stopped, and went to do something about it.

But once the class was finished and everyone had gone home, she tidied up by rote, her mind a thousand miles away. Or at least a hundred or so, where Heikon's Aerie was.

Why are you here, when you could be where he is?

Why indeed? she thought.

She went up to the roof. Darkness had fully fallen, and the clouds had pulled back for the first time in a week, showing the stars. It was a beautiful night to fly.

She let her cashmere wrap fall from her shoulders. With darkness to cover her, she shifted, embracing her dragon as they became one.

There had better not be one word out of you, she told her dragon sternly as her wings flexed, beating strongly downward, sending two of the patio chairs tumbling as she took to the sky.

We fly, her dragon said, in agreement or possibly just distracted with only one thing on its one-track reptile mind. *Can we hunt along the way?*

Perhaps a little. But the important thing is getting where we're going.

I know, her dragon said, and it didn't quite acknowledge the importance of her mission ... but it didn't argue about it, either.

93

HEIKON

"So are you going to talk about what's bothering you, or sulk around the Aerie driving everyone insane?" Anjelica said tartly.

"I am not *sulking*." Heikon clipped carefully at the tip of a pear branch. It was night, but floodlights illuminated the garden. Since all their supplies had to be shipped in, they provided as much as possible of their own produce, including growing out-of-season tropical fruit in large greenhouses. There were a number of fruit-breeding and tree-splicing projects that Heikon and some of the other interested dragons were working on, to increase their local produce yields.

"Cousin ..." Anjelica sighed and leaned against the trunk of the tree. She was his cousin once or twice removed, one of the Aerie's several wingless Asian dragons. Anyone else he would have thrown out, but she was almost as old as he was, and extremely stubborn. "It's *her*, isn't it?"

"Don't be absurd." How could it have been a mere 24 hours since he'd last seen Esme? She was in his every thought. He had awakened this morning feeling as if he should be able to reach out and touch her—had, in fact, rolled over before he woke up enough to realize that she wasn't in his bed.

Would never be in his bed, the way things were going.

Anjelica huffed at the look on his face. "If she's getting to you that much, Cousin, go to her."

"I have no idea what you're talking about."

"If you want her, you have to go get her," Anjelica said impatiently. "What, do you think she's just going to drop out of the sky into your lap?"

Which was the exact point when Esme's dragon, with impeccable if accidental timing, landed in the garden with an earth-shaking thump.

Heikon dropped the gardening shears. Anjelica jumped and began instinctively to shift. "No!" Heikon said, catching her arm. "That's a friend. Esme, have a little mercy on my security staff."

"Oh," Anjelica said, through a mouthful of fangs. She relaxed back to her her human form. "Sorry, Lady Esmerelda. I didn't recognize you for a minute there. Didn't the sentries challenge you?"

"I saw them," Esme's dragon said in her melodious voice. She towered above them, and Heikon took a moment to appreciate the grandeur of her wings and scales before she dwindled to normal human size. It looked like she'd come straight from her dance studio; she was still wearing a swishy dancing dress, this one pale violet, very striking with her red hair. "And I flew right by them. Really, Heikon, leaving juveniles in charge of your perimeter?"

"They have to learn somehow. I wasn't expecting you to stop by and test my defenses," Heikon said. He was torn between embarrassment and the almost overwhelming urge to grab her and kiss her.

"From what I can see," she said, a bit stiffly, "*your* defenses are just fine. Your security, however, leaves something to be desired."

Anjelica cleared her throat as the air in the garden became frosty. "I'll have a word with them. And welcome back to the Aerie, Lady Esmerelda. Will you be staying the night? I can have a room prepared."

"I'm not sure," Esme said, and for the first time she looked hesitant.

"Get a room ready," Heikon told Anjelica. She nodded, shifted, and flew off in the corkscrew way of the wingless dragons.

They were left alone in the floodlit garden. The clear, cool artificial light picked out the edges of every curl, brought definition to the lace edging on the dress's neckline, above her full breasts.

She was unbearably beautiful. And she was here.

"Esme," he said gently.

"Don't 'Esme' me. I flew all this way and I find you *gardening?*" Without waiting for an answer, she strolled around the fruit tree, looking at it. "What is this?"

"It's a graft of different varieties of pear," he said, seizing gratefully onto the conversational topic. "I've been trying to develop some different types that will withstand our harsh climate here in the mountains. It's not the best climate for agriculture."

"I had ... forgotten, I think, that this was something you used to love." She looked up at the tree's spreading branches, her face half in shadow.

"There's so much I've forgotten about you, too." Maybe it was the wrong thing to say, but all he had for her now, all he could give her, was honesty. "There's a lot to relearn, but I'd really like to try, if I can."

"You left," she said, looking up at the tree.

"You asked me to."

"I was expecting you to come back."

He wasn't sure what to say to that. She turned to look at him, her lashes casting long shadows across her cheekbones.

"I ... apologize," he said.

Esme shook her head. "I don't want apologies. I want ..." She took a deep breath, and looked around at the gardens, not finishing the sentence.

"You know," he began cautiously, hardly daring to hope, "the gardens are finest at night."

"I'd think you wouldn't be able to see anything."

"That's what the lights are for." And he offered an elbow.

There was a pause—the longest of his life, while his heart teetered on a fulcrum. And then she took his elbow with the slightest of smiles.

They strolled through the multilevel garden, his passion for centuries. Heikon had put great thought into the placement of every bush and tree—only to have most of the original garden ripped out during Braun's tenure as clanlord, including irreplaceable trees that were hundreds of years old. He could never fix that. But they had replanted and rebuilt. The damage from the fight with the gargoyles was also being repaired, though they passed draped plastic sheeting covering the worst of it, and spindly saplings starting to establish themselves where full-sized trees had once stood.

But that was the way of gardens, wasn't it? They were never truly finished. Heikon had yet to meet a single gardener who considered their garden complete. It was the nature of all living organisms to grow and change, and a garden was made up of living things. Even if you could eventually achieve the mythical state of a complete, perfect garden, the plants themselves would still suffer attacks of beetle and fungus, would die in a harsh winter or fail to thrive as their neighboring shade tree grew too wide for their sun-loving leaves.

Gardening, Heikon believed, taught you flexibility. It taught you that not everything was in your control. He sometimes thought that his comparatively young and reckless counterpart—Darius Keegan, lord of the Keegan clan, father of Esme's daughter Melody—would have been a happier and less controlling person if he, too, had taken up gardening as a hobby.

Of course, Darius had eventually learned to bend and change because of his children and grandchildren ... and his cats. Heikon couldn't help smiling at the thought.

"What's funny?" Esme asked quietly. She had walked in silence, looking around at the floodlit flowers and the fairy lights draped in the bushes, but he hadn't felt the need to break the silence with words. The comfort between them was more than enough.

"I was thinking about Darius," Heikon admitted. "Believe it or not."

She snorted a short laugh. "You're walking in a garden with me, thinking about my ex?"

"Okay, it sounds weird when you put it that way ..."

"Heikon." She stopped him with a hand on his chest. They were under one of the garden's handful of remaining full-sized trees, a spreading willow with its branches draped with fairy lights twinkling like captive stars. "Don't forget, it was you who once reminded me that we've both lived a long, full life. Taken lovers. Raised children. Before what happened with us, before I knew what a true mate feels like, I would have welcomed you as a lover, had we both wanted it."

"And now?" he asked, all but holding his breath. She was so near. It would be the matter of an instant to take her in his arms.

"Perhaps we can't be mates, not as we once were. But ..." She tilted her face up to his. "I feel as if it's possible we might be more than lovers. Do you?"

His dragon, uncharacteristically, was silent. It wasn't rising with joy at the presence of his mate, as it had done before. But he felt no resistance, no disapproval.

"Perhaps," he breathed, and he pulled her to him, and took her mouth with his own.

ESME

I f this was kissing without the mate bond, it was probably just as well, because a kiss fed with that underlying channel of soul-deep connection would have melted her.

They kissed and kissed, and she couldn't even remember when his hands in her hair dislodged the pins—but it was down, falling all around her, stirred in the nighttime breeze.

"Are you—" he breathed against her lips, and she whispered back, "Yes."

The branches of the willow tree, woven through with lights, were like a bower all around them, shutting out curious eyes. Heikon drew her down onto the soft moss under the tree. He stripped out of his jacket and spread it like a blanket.

"Will anyone—"

"Anjelica will keep them away. I think she read the situation better than I did."

His undershirt followed the jacket, and then she was finally able to run her hands across the planes of the sculpted body she'd dreamed about for twenty years.

Every touch seemed to ignite the fire blazing between them. She didn't want to hope, not after all this time—but was it *possible* ... could this ultimate connection repair the mate bond?

Only one way to find out, she thought, and gave herself over completely to the heat blazing in her, the hot well of need between her legs.

Her dress followed his shirt, and then it was skin on skin, moving against each other in the semi-dark. The sweat-slick friction of their bodies—his hands guiding her hips—her mouth sealed against his—

They were one being, united in frantic, passionate need. Twenty years of separation built rapidly toward a blazing climax, and she shuddered through the throes of an orgasm like nothing she'd experienced in two decades.

They collapsed together, limbs twined around each other. The fairy lights cast white and blue patterns across his skin.

With sated bliss purling through her, she opened herself wide, reaching out, straining for what she had once felt whenever she was near him.

Is it possible ...

And for a moment she almost thought—

But there was nothing there. She felt relaxed and good, but only in the normal, post-sex kind of way. Whatever this consummation had done for both of them, it had done nothing for the mate bond.

Esme turned her face into his shoulder.

"Esme," he said, shocked, as her hot tears soaked his skin. "Esme. Dear Esme." He held her, rocked her, and then drew back and took her face in his hands. "What's wrong? Wasn't it —wasn't it good for you?"

"No!" she said, shocked that he would even think that. "No, no, please—it was good. So good. I missed ..." She pulled in a shuddering breath, and tears sprang to her eyes for a new reason, splintering the fairy lights to a kaleidoscope of bright splinters. The raw truth was pulled out of her, one painful word at a time. "I missed you *so much.*"

"Oh, Esme." He buried his face in her neck. "I missed you too. So much. *So* much."

She clung to him, feeling him against every part of her, and in that moment, she decided. *So what* if the mate bond wasn't back? *So what* if all they ever had was an ordinary love between the human parts of them?

It was so much more than most people ever got. So much more than she'd had before she met him.

If the world wouldn't give them what they wanted, maybe they'd just have to take it for themselves.

The night air was growing chilly on their naked skin. They dressed under the tree, and Esme opted to carry her shoes rather than trying to walk in them. The garden paths weren't friendly to high-heeled shoes, but the rounded gravel was smooth enough on her bare feet.

"We could go flying under the moon," Heikon said, and then he laughed quietly. She loved that laugh, a deep warm chuckle that seemed to go straight through her. "Or we could go up to the Aerie, where there are soft beds and hot cocoa. You know, I think I might be getting old."

"If you are, then so am I, because that sounds wonderful to me."

"I know you don't want apologies," he said as they climbed a flight of stone steps from one garden level to the next. "But I *am* sorry that I didn't come back tonight. That you had to hunt me down."

"*I'm* not," she said. "If you had, I would never have had a chance to decide for myself if this was something I was willing to fight for. Sometimes you have to feel yourself on the edge of losing something before you realize it's worth keeping."

She stopped there, because she could feel the gulf widening between them again at the reminder of everything they *had* lost, through twenty years' silence.

But she could admit to herself now that it wasn't just Heikon. Twenty years. She could have come back. She could have searched for him. She could have decided not to take the severing of the mate bond as an ending, but rather an opportunity to fight.

I think we both have a lot to learn about fighting for what we want.

It was all too easy when you were a shifter to think that love would be delivered to you on a silver platter. Someday you'd find your mate and then things would be simple. Right?

It had never been simple with them. Apparently it was never going to be.

But wasn't the best hunt the most difficult, and the most rewarding dance the one that had taken the longest to learn?

"Heikon?" she said, and he turned to her. She was used to being the tallest person in the room, as she usually was among humans; it was strange and wonderful to be around someone who was slightly taller than she was. "Have you ever looked into getting the mate bond restored? I mean, is it something that could possibly be done?"

"I ..." he began, then fell quiet, and climbed a few steps in silence. They emerged onto a patio surrounded by ornamental bushes, with a wide veranda opening onto it. "I sought out stories," he said at last, giving her a hand up onto the veranda. "It's such a rare thing to lose the mate bond that there are no reliable records of it. I hoped an answer could be found in the lore of our kind."

The veranda, like the garden, was decorated with lights. She remembered now how the Aerie, back in its heyday twenty years ago, used to shine like a Christmas ornament from afar. The one other time she'd been here, they had just suffered the gargoyle attack and the mountain was in a state of emergency. Now it was starting to glitter and shine again.

The fairy-tale effect was suddenly spoiled by the clatter of tiny toenails on the floor and the whisk of something past her legs, under the edge of her skirt. Esme yelped and jumped. Her dragon's predator instincts took over, and she whirled around and pounced, pinning whatever it was before it had a chance to get away. Her shoes went flying, forgotten. She straightened up holding a small, squirming, reptilian shape that nibbled at her fingers and then abruptly shifted into a plump toddler, about two years old, with wide dark eyes and curly dark hair.

"Pixie," Heikon sighed. "Give her here."

"Nope, I caught her, she's mine now," Esme said. Pixie giggled and shoved her fist in her mouth, and Esme was suddenly, wildly nostalgic for Melody as an infant. Becoming a grandmother might make her feel about a thousand years old, but she couldn't *wait* for grandchildren.

Heikon collected her shoes, and she carried Pixie across the veranda, occasionally flipping the little girl upside down to make her squeal with laughter.

At the door leading inside, they were met by a panting, wide-eyed teenage girl. "Where are they? Oh, thank goodness!" She took Pixie back from Esme, and peered past her. "Did you see another one out there?"

"Which one?" Heikon asked.

"Feodran! It's always Feo. He's going to be such a trouble-maker when he grows up." She heaved an exasperated sigh. "He's a troublemaker now. I should put a bell on him."

Seeing her up close in better light, Esme realized that the

girl was not a teenager after all. She could easily be in her late twenties or early thirties, perhaps much older since she was probably also a dragon. She was just small and baby-faced. Esme hadn't met very many dragons who were extremely short in their human form, but this one was barely over five feet. From the way she was cuddling Pixie, she was probably their mother.

"I can do better than that." Heikon looked around, checking for clearance, but the hallway was large and wide, designed for dragons. "Step back."

He shifted, and suddenly his vast gunmetal dragon filled the hallway. "Feodran!" The order rang out in his deep dragon's voice, reverberating off the walls and echoing with alpha command.

A moment later, from some unseen alcove above them, a tiny dragon pounced onto Heikon's great spined back with a high-pitched yipping noise of delight.

Heikon shifted back, twisting as he did so to catch the little dragon. "Here," he said, handing Feodran back to his mother.

"Thank you," she said gratefully, trying to hang onto both of them. "No, settle down, it's bedtime. Feo, *stop* getting your sister so exited. It's very nice to see you again, Lady Esmerelda!" she said over her shoulder as she hurried off.

"How does she know me when I don't know her?" But Esme could answer the question for herself. "Oh. She was one of the fighting dragons in the battle against the gargoyles, wasn't she? I met so many that day, and then many more later when I was tending the wounded. I'm impressed, by the way, at how well you've rebuilt in such a short period of time."

"It's one thing we have regrettably gotten a lot of practice at, rebuilding." Heikon picked up her shoes. "That was my granddaughter Kana, by the way. I would have introduced you, but—"

"No, as a mother myself, I completely understand. Anyway, I expect I'm going to need a chart to keep all your grandchildren and great-grandchildren straight."

"You're in luck, then." Heikon smiled as he opened a door to a flight of stairs. "One of the great-nieces actually did make one on her computer. I'm sure she'll show it to you if you like."

The stairs took them to an extensive kitchen complex, all quiet now, shut down for the night. They went through the edge of it, past enormous ovens and refrigerators large enough to supply a restaurant. Esme noticed a large kitchen-duty whiteboard on the wall, with a sketched-in calendar and dozens of names.

"If you want something to eat, there are always snacks around," Heikon said. "Or we could cook something."

"Not really. But it's nice to know it's an option." As they left the kitchens and climbed more stairs, she added, "I'm starting to feel that the thing I'm going to need most isn't your genealogy chart, it's a map. Or do you have those too?"

"Not really as such. Too much of a security risk. I'll be happy to show you around, though. And of course ..."

He paused by an open balcony. The mountain had many of those, she'd noticed, open to the air with folding wooden shutters that could be pulled across to shut out the winter cold. Some of them were boarded up now, some of the windows made smaller for defense, but there were still many places to leap off and take wing.

"... if you want to fly," Heikon said quietly, "you can fly whenever you want."

This was a place built by and for dragons. It had never really hit her before, not in quite this way. She'd lived for so long among the humans that it was a strange and wonderful feeling to think that she could just be herself here. The ceilings were high enough to shift whenever she wanted. She could step off the balcony and fly at any time if she felt like it, not having to worry about waiting for darkness or foggy weather and making sure humans didn't see her.

"I think I'll save that for later," she said, slipping her hand into his. "Right now I'm more interested in bed."

"Yes. Indeed." His voice went low, shivering pleasantly through her. "There'll be a room made up for you on the guest level, and you're welcome to it. But if you'd prefer something else, my bed is large, and I'd be honored if you'd share it."

She tightened her grip on his hand. "I'd love to."

ESME

E sme woke, blissful and lazy with sleep, to the sun streaming across her face. She turned her head to the side—had she forgotten to close the blinds? No ... there were no blinds, only windows standing open to the sky. A breeze brushed her face. And then she remembered where she was.

She sat up, naked, and looked to the bed beside her. It was empty.

"Heikon?"

She got out of bed and reached for the robe draped over a chair in convenient reach. Heikon's chambers were enormous. A dozen dragons could have shifted in here—could have, and probably had. A balcony ran the entire length of the room, with wide doors standing open to let the fresh air in.

The robe was a silken kimono in her colors, gold and green. Esme belted it around her waist and wandered out onto the balcony. The view was stunning. Heikon's quarters were near the top of the mountain, and it seemed as if the entire world lay before her, spread out in a patchwork of greens and browns and hazy, distant blues. There were few signs of human occupation, just a few distantly visible traceries of roads, hair-fine from here, and perhaps the odd blocky square of what might be far-off farm fields or pastures. But other than that, everything she saw was wild land and the modifications that Heikon had made to it.

Which were extensive. She'd forgotten how much of the mountain was occupied. It was really a little town, with terraced gardens and fields marching down the side of the mountain. Heikon's personal gardens were at the top of the terracing, and below those, farm fields and sheep pastures. She vaguely remembered all of this from when she was here before, but now she looked at it with new eyes, thinking about how much work it must take to live here. She could see some of Heikon's clan below her; someone was running a tractor, and several of the teenage kids were tending the sheep.

More than anything else, Heikon's clan was like a big farm family. Her own clan enjoyed the understated luxury of their mountain chalets, and Darius, as she recalled, had gone for opulence all the way, building himself an enormous mansion with a staff of servants. But Heikon, it seemed, had gone for isolation and independence over wealth and luxury. Even though they could easily fly to nearby towns in just an hour or two, it must be a life of hard work out here, with occasional deprivation; all their supplies aside from what they made themselves must be brought in from nearby towns.

"Esme?" Heikon called from within the room.

"Out here!"

A moment later, he appeared with a breakfast tray. "There you are. Feel like a morning flight?"

"I'm more curious what you have there. Is that coffee I smell?"

It was indeed, a fine-quality roast, and there were also breakfast rolls and omelets. Heikon set the tray down on one of several wooden tables on the balcony, and they ate. It was simple fare, but filling and good, and there was plenty of it.

"This is mostly local," Heikon said. "Eggs from our chickens, peppers and tomatoes from the greenhouses—we keep them running all winter long for fresh salad greens. Even the nuts in the rolls are locally harvested. The flour comes in from outside, though in theory we could grow it here—we have a mill, down on the lower levels of the mountain, water-powered. We operated it sometimes to grind barley. Some things are much easier to import, like flour and sugar, tea and coffee ... but I try to keep an eye on the possibility of growing them ourselves if our supply lines got cut and we needed to."

She wasn't sure if he was trying to impress her or simply waxing enthusiastic, but, well, it *was* impressive, what they'd built here. "Do you think it's likely that you'd be cut off like that?"

"Not really, but what if we were? There are almost two hundred people who live here, most of them descended from me or from my parents' relatives, as well as their mates and occasionally their mates' relatives who came along."

"That's a lot," Esme said, surprised. "I didn't know your clan was that big."

"We're bigger than most clans because we're careful. We keep to ourselves, and we provide most of what we need. And we maintain our ties to other clans carefully, trying not to antagonize them."

"Like when you sent an assassin to kill Darius's daughter-in-law?" Esme asked archly.

"That was an exception," Heikon said with great dignity. "I didn't know she was mated to his son, and I thought she was involved with the coup against me."

"Yes. That." Esme looked down at the view again, the peaceful serenity of the landscape. "It's hard to believe there was fighting going on here so recently. Everything seems so calm."

"I hope never to see fighting on my clan lands again," Heikon said. He refreshed his coffee cup from the steaming pot on the tray. His face looked troubled. "Esme ... would you care to take a flight with me a little later? There's someone I would very much like you to meet."

"From what I can tell, there are a lot of people around here to meet. I'd better have that great-niece of yours print out your family tree."

She smiled, and Heikon returned it, but in a distant kind of way. "No, they're not local. I *do* want you to meet my clan, but most importantly, I'd like you to meet my mother."

His mother. The one who'd known he wasn't dead, when even Esme didn't. "All right," she said, guarded. "Tell me something. If your mother is still alive, how are you the clan-lord, rather than her?"

"Mother wasn't interested. She lives alone, well, except for ..." Uncharacteristically, he hesitated, seeming unsure. "There's something I'd like to share with you. Something I haven't told anyone else. But I need to take you to Mother's place first."

"Yes, of course." She looked down at herself, realizing that she was wearing a borrowed kimono, had no clean clothes, and hadn't even brushed her hair. "Uh, first I should clean up a bit. I didn't come here prepared to meet your parents, Heikon!"

"Calmly," he soothed. "I'm sure Mother will like you."

"That's hardly the point. How would *you* enjoy being whisked overseas with no preparation to meet my parents?"

"Hmm. I see your point. I could perhaps borrow some things from Anjelica for you? I think she's about your height."

"That would be great," she said. "And point me to the shower, if you don't mind."

One thing the mountain had was hot water and plenty of it. Shortly she joined Heikon on the balcony, feeling a bit awkward in Anjelica's black and violet flight leathers.

"Doesn't this woman own any normal clothes?"

"We both thought you'd prefer something a bit more formal than the jeans she wears for gardening," Heikon said dryly. "And she doesn't own anything with a skirt." He gave her a long, appreciative look. "Trust me, this is an *extremely* flattering look on you."

Esme looked down at herself. She had twisted her hair into a thick braid, coiled on top of her head, and examining herself earlier in the bedroom mirrors, she had to admit that the effect combined with Anjelica's leather body armor was a very striking one. She looked like some kind of warrior maiden, prepared to head into battle.

Hopefully it would have an equally impressive effect on Heikon's mother. Esme could only imagine what the woman was like. She had met very few truly old dragons; they mostly kept to themselves. Her own parents were both still alive, but neither of them was much older than Heikon.

"Ready?" Heikon asked, and she nodded.

He leaped from the balcony, shifting in midair. His dragon uncoiled, enormous and blue-gray, gleaming in the sun like polished metal.

Esme followed suit, feeling the wind catch her.

Finally! her dragon trumpeted inside her head. *We hunt! We fly!*

Heikon flew in a lazy circle, and she settled into formation with him, flying just below his wingtip so he could show her where they were going. It felt so easy and natural that they might have done it a thousand times before.

As if they were meant to fly together, she thought as they

straightened out and soared together toward distant blue peaks.

◿

T he last time Esme had flown this far had been ... hmm, the last time she was at the Aerie, probably, on their ill-fated hunt. Hopefully today would have a better ending.

It felt wonderful to stretch her wings like this, with little fear of anyone seeing them. The sun was warm on her back, the breeze delightfully cool. They circled above a small herd of elk, but flew on without hunting. It would slow them down and burden them needlessly. They could always do it on the way back, if they felt like it.

The land beneath them grew even rougher and wilder. She'd thought Heikon's mountain was remote, but this was true wilderness, unbroken by anything but an scattered hunter's cabin here, a winding dirt road there.

"This part is all national forest," Heikon told her. His dragon's voice thrummed like a symphony. "Humans come here, but rarely. And large tracts of land are privately owned by my family. It will never be developed."

It made her miss her native Alps, and as they flew she told him about her adventures in the mountains as a young dragon, hunting ibex and chamois in wildflower-decked meadows.

She had forgotten how delightful it was to fly with someone when you were so much in sync.

They flew through a steep-walled canyon, so narrow they had to twist their wings sideways to avoid hitting the cliff-sides, and came out in a broad valley. The change was abrupt, from absolute wilderness to a place that had clearly been cultivated for some time. Even the trees had been thinned and cultivated in pleasing symmetry. Gardens unrolled below them in great, colorful banks of flowers. Esme looked around for signs of habitation, but other than the gardens, she saw none until Heikon changed course and winged toward the top of the cliffs surrounding the valley. And then she saw it, a tidy stone house perched on the clifftop.

Just in front of the house was an enormous patio made of native stone, placed in appealing, abstract patterns. Esme guessed this was intended as a sort of dragon landing pad; it was right on the edge of the cliff, making it easy to depart by diving off and catching an updraft. And, indeed, Heikon landed on the patio and shifted as soon as his feet touched down. Esme followed suit.

The woman who came to greet them from the house was tiny and shockingly old. Esme wasn't sure if she'd ever seen a dragon with such visible signs of age, and it made her think of the humans she'd come to think of as "her" old people. Despite her age, Heikon's mother held herself ramrod-straight. Her hair, pulled back in a neat bun and secured with a jeweled clasp, was snow white.

"Esme, this is Okiko, my mother," Heikon said, taking his mother's hands. "Mother, this is Esmerelda of the Lavigna clan."

"Ma'am," Esme greeted her politely, with a bow.

"You must be special, for my son to bring you here." Okiko turned to her son. "Don't tell me—is she your mate?"

Heikon started to answer, then hesitated—looking toward Esme, letting her choose how to explain their unusual situation.

"No," Esme said, and she saw him deflate a little. But it was true. She wasn't going to lie about it. "But I care very much for your son," she went on, and hope ignited in Heikon's face. "I would like to become closer."

"Hmm," was Okiko's response to this. "Have you eaten?"

Since they weren't particularly hungry after their full breakfast, she served them tea and small, colorful cookies in the garden. It was even more peaceful and idyllic than Heikon's mountain, and she was hyper-aware of Heikon's presence, the brush of his hand as he passed the cookie plate to her.

But there was also something else. As they sipped tea and made polite conversation, Esme kept sensing undercurrents passing between mother and son. It was not telepathy exactly, but there was some kind of conversation going on between them, conveyed in frowns and meaningful glances.

When Okiko went into the house to refresh their tea, brushing off their offers to help her, Esme leaned close and murmured, "Okay, something's going on here. You didn't just bring me out here to have tea with your mother, did you?"

Heikon's smile was more like a grimace. "You are perceptive."

"More like I'm not a fool. Why are we really here, Heikon?"

Rather than answering, he rose, and held out a courtly hand. Esme allowed him to help her up. Then he went to intercept his mother at the door. They spoke too quietly for Esme to hear, and by the time she got there, his mother had set down the tea things and picked up a pair of gardening shears.

"Come find me afterwards," she said. "I must show you the new rose cultivar I've obtained. It is incredibly rare; only a few specimens exist in the world."

Heikon kissed her cheek. "I look forward to it."

Okiko went off into the garden, and Esme gave Heikon a look that was both curious and suspicious.

"Come," he said. "What I am about to show you is known to none except me and my mother. It cannot be known or I risk losing everything I have. It is, perhaps, my greatest secret, certainly my greatest weakness. Will you swear to keep my secret?"

"I swear," she said, meeting his eyes.

He went not into the house, but to the edge of the cliff. Now wildly curious, Esme followed him. When he leaped off and shifted, she was a mere step behind him.

Even so, she was shocked to lose sight of him. She'd expected to see him soar across the valley. Instead, he was—where? She swooped in a low circle in midair, trying to see where he'd gone. It wasn't like a dragon was an easy thing to hide!

And then she glimpsed movement on the cliff. Heikon's long neck and spiked dragon's head poked out from what she would have sworn was sheer cliffside.

"This way, my love."

Love. He had never used that word before, and she sensed a sudden, startled pulling away; he hadn't meant to use it now. But the emotions were always closer to the surface when their dragons were dominant.

Shaken, she flew toward him, and found a cleverly hidden entrance in the rocks. It was invisible from afar, and even up close, it hardly looked big enough for a dragon—but when she folded her wings and slithered after him, she just fit inside.

Once they were through the hidden entrance, the passage narrowed still further, forcing her to shift. Heikon was waiting for her a little way along, with a flashlight in his hand.

"How cozy," she said, looking around them. "What's down here? Is it—"

She broke off as the most likely possibility occurred to her. Was *this* the Heart of his hoard, then? Perhaps she'd been wrong about the cherry-tree grove.

And if he shared his with her, did he expect her to share her own?

It was not a terrible thought. Once she'd looked forward to showing him her secret sea cave in Greece. The mental image of having Heikon there made a strange thrill go through her. It was, in its own way, more intimate than sex.

But then he answered with a strange bleakness in his voice.

"I'm not sure if I can explain," he said. "You have to see."

Now she was even more curious. They were under his mother's house. What could be here that would bring that tense edge into his tone?

She followed him down the passageway. It seemed to be a natural crack in the rocks that had been enlarged—crudely and in haste, from what she could tell, putting it at odds with the meticulous planning that was evident in the house and garden above.

Abruptly it widened out into a large chamber. There was a glassed-in skylight in the ceiling, shedding light. From down here she could see branches crowding over the skylight's glass dome. It must be hidden in the garden or woods.

But she had little attention to spare the room's architecture, because in this room, there was a dragon.

It was one of the biggest she'd ever seen, at least as big as Heikon, if not larger. The dragon filled the room, curled like a sleeping cat, tail hooked over its nose. Its eyes were closed. Asleep .... or dead? There was no sign of breathing, no rise and fall of the scaly sides. This dragon was black and green, a combination that created a slightly poisonous effect, as if the lurid green stripes might ooze something toxic.

And then she noticed that both of the dragon's front ankles, as well as its neck, wore heavy iron cuffs. Enormous chains, each link as big as two of her fists together, went from the cuffs to iron rings pounded into the walls. Its back legs were hidden under its wings, but she could see another pair of chains coming from under the wings, so its back legs were cuffed too.

These cuffs were evidently designed not only to hold the dragon but to stop it from shifting. The cuffs were obviously too large for a human neck or wrists, but it would take some extremely skilled shifting to keep from being pulled apart if someone tried to shift back while wearing them. It would be possible, she thought, but not easy.

"Who ..."

"My brother," Heikon said quietly. "Braun."

He reached out as if to touch Braun's massive head, then pulled his hand back.

"Is he dead?" Esme asked.

"No," Heikon said. "What's been done to him is what he did to me, without meaning to. A dose of concentrated drag-onsbane, not quite strong enough to kill, puts a dragon into a suspended state. Heartbeat, breathing, metabolism, all slowed to almost nothing. In my case, it saved my life. In Braun's case, it keeps him comatose, unable to threaten me or those I hold dear."

Esme circled around the edge of the room, stepping care-fully over a wing. As far as she could tell, there were no dragon-sized exits. Braun must have been brought here in human form, and could not leave without shifting back.

"You've allowed everyone to believe he's dead," she said.

"I know. It was necessary. When I came back after being gone for twenty years, Braun had alienated most of the clan with his cruel, heavy-handed rule, but he still had some followers. I had to take him out of the picture so they would have no choice but to fall in line behind me. There was some bloodshed, but nothing like the open warfare we'd have had if there were two competing rivals for the head of the clan."

"Wouldn't it have been easier to just kill him?"

"He's my brother," Heikon said. "Yes, it would have been easier. In the heat of battle, I might have been able to do it. But I managed to get the drop on him, took him down before he had a chance to fight, and then ..." He shook his head. "Well. You see."

"The story I heard was that you had Braun and his inner circle executed."

Heikon shook his head again. "A necessary lie. Everyone who died was killed in the initial fighting. But a show of strength was necessary. After twenty years of Braun, rule by the strong was all that my clan understands. So yes, I put that story around, to discourage any attempts to knock me off the clanlord's throne again."

"Peace by the sword," Esme murmured.

"And peace is what we have," Heikon said. "All because of a necessary lie to prevent further killing."

"What if he escapes?"

"That's why I asked Mother to guard him. She was the one person I trusted to do it."

Privately, Esme wondered if she would trust herself to guard her dearly beloved child. Of course, the idea of Melody being accused of terrible crimes was so unthinkable that she could not even entertain it as a hypothetical possibility.

"Do you see why no one must learn of this?" A note of desperation slipped into Heikon's voice. "Peace in my clan depends on it. If anyone knew of Braun's survival, there are certain factions that I fear would try to slip in and release him."

She turned back and looked at him past the curve of Braun's great wing. "And yet you trust me to keep this secret for you."

"I trust you." The words slipped out on a breath. "I trust

119

you with my life and my heart—and with a secret that could destroy all I hold dear."

She had been wrong. Offering her the Heart of his hoard, the key to his very life, was a small thing compared to this. Because this was a secret much bigger than just one dragon. This was, as he'd said, a secret on which the survival of his clan was balanced.

And he had given it to her, with open hands.

"I'll keep your secret," she said, for all the good it would do. What use were words in a situation like this? She could only prove her trustworthiness day by day, holding his secret for a lifetime.

But she saw him relax, as if some hidden tension had eased out of him at her promise. The words mattered to him, she realized. They mattered a lot.

She picked her way back to him, carefully not touching Braun. It was eerie; the huge dragon still looked dead to her. She trusted that Heikon was right that he was still alive, but seeing it was different from hearing about it. She could see why Heikon had felt he needed to bring her here.

And it also brought home to her what he'd gone through when his brother had poisoned him.

"How long was it like this for you?" she asked gently as they left the cave and entered the narrow, twisting passage back to the cliff.

"I don't know. Years, I think. It's all a haze. I came back to myself very slowly. But," he added with a brief, tight smile, "if not for that, I'd have died. The cold of the lake in which I fell, combined with the poison that felled me, kept me from dying completely until my body could heal itself."

"I thought you had. Died, that is."

It was the first time she had really allowed herself to feel her grief since those very early days. The realization that Heikon had been killed—as she'd thought—had utterly devastated her. But she'd fought it down because she had to be there for Melody, and then the knowledge that he was alive, and her anger over having been lied to, had flattened the memory of the pain, washed it away in the kind of anger you could only have against someone who was still alive.

Someone you loved.

Now the memory of that overwhelming grief hit her again full force. It was a grief she could have easily drowned in. And then she'd blamed him for the pain she'd felt, but ...

But he was a victim too. And she hadn't really let herself think of it. Or remember the devastation, the agony of knowing he'd been there, and then he wasn't—

"Esme?" His arm went around her in the narrow confines of the passage. "I know this is a lot to take in—"

"It's not that." She turned and put her arms around him, flashlight and all. "It's just ... all of it. *All* of it. You're not dead."

"No," he said, and buried his face in her hair. "I'm not."

"You lied to me."

"I know. I shouldn't have."

"No," she said into his chest. "You shouldn't have. But I ..." She drew in a shuddering breath. "I should have asked. I should have tried harder to find you."

"You didn't know—"

"But it doesn't matter!" she cried, looking up at his face. With his arms around her, the flashlight pointed at the floor, all she could see was a wash of shadows and the warm gleam of his eyes. "It doesn't *matter*. We were mates. We were partners. You left me, but I—I also left you, and I *shouldn't* have, I ..."

"Shhh." He held her, kissed her forehead, her damp cheek. "We've both done things we shouldn't have."

If they were still what they'd once been, she would have been able to feel him now through the mate bond. But there was still the warm support of his arms around her, his body against hers; his quick mind and subtle sense of humor and the companionship he offered. She had lost him once and gotten him back. Who was she to decry her luck and reject what she'd been offered, just because it wasn't exactly what it had been before?

"Have you ever heard of kintsugi?" she asked, pulling far enough away to look into his shadowed face.

"Kintsugi?"

"Yes. It's the art of mending broken teacups with gold. You take something that's been broken, and repair it with a fine seam of gold along the broken line. It's not just trying to fix it as if it was never broken, a beautiful lie as if the damage never happened. It's taking the brokenness and making *art* out of it."

He smiled down at her, a beloved shadow in the near-dark. "Actually, it's more of a philosophical statement about the impermanence of existence and the inevitability of—"

"Heikon?"

"Mmm?"

"Shut up. I'm making a point."

"Yes, ma'am," he said, and there was such a wealth of warmth and affection in it that filled her heart and brimmed over.

I don't care where we started out or what we could have been. We have a second chance now, and I'm making gold out of this.

She turned her face up and kissed him.

ESME

The next few weeks were the happiest of Esme's life. She and Heikon divided their time between the Aerie and Esme's dance studio. Outwardly, for the most part, their lives went on as before. She taught her classes, though she'd cut back to three or four days a week so she didn't have to shuffle back and forth between the city and the Aerie quite so often. Heikon still spent the majority of his time with his gardens and his noisy, bustling clan.

But it was a rare night anymore when either of them slept alone, ate alone. He slept over at her apartment so often that they'd begun keeping spare clothes for him there, and she had packed up a suitcase to take to the Aerie so she could stop borrowing other people's things. His toothbrush had moved in next to hers, and she had a spread of makeup in his bathroom.

She had become a fixture at Corcoran clan breakfasts, just as Heikon had started to spend so much time in her neighborhood that people recognized him there, and asked after him.

They wandered the streets together, and she took him to

all her favorite restaurants. He bought beautiful glass hair ornaments and silk scarves for her at the little local artisan shops, and rarely left without some toy or other from the independent toy store down the street to take back to the children at the Aerie.

And, in the mountains, they went flying together, wings spread under the sun, unafraid of prying human eyes. He showed her his gardens, displaying rare plants for her as if they were jewels, and picked flowers for her to braid into her hair.

He even took her to the sakura grove that she remembered from so long ago. It was not as it had once been, with the trees towering up the canyon walls. Braun, he told her, had cut down all the trees, and burned the rest. When Heikon had returned from his exile and reclaimed his mountain, he had found a brush-choked wilderness in place of the old cherry trees.

But throughout Heikon's long life, ever since he had established the grove with cherry seeds his mother had brought across the sea from Japan, he'd had a tradition of giving a small potted cherry seedling to each person in his clan when they traveled. It was for luck, and for a connection to the clan they'd left behind. So his trees were scattered across the world, and when he reclaimed the mountain and began to repair his gardens, it had been a small matter to obtain seeds from those many far-scattered trees, and even recover some of the young trees themselves, and bring them back to rebuild the grove.

The replanted grove was still young, slim trees spreading their tender leaves toward the sky, most of them no higher than Esme's waist. But she thought she was learning to see what Heikon saw, the potential inherent in each young plant, the minds-eye vision of what they would look like in full flower. The grove was not going to be exactly as it had been before, but it would be beautiful. It was beautiful now.

Mended with gold.

~

Quietly, on the side, Esme looked into draconic lore for any information on how to mend a broken mate bond.

It was not an easy thing to research. As Heikon had said, it was a vanishingly rare event, so uncommon that it was not recorded anywhere. She had to ask, quietly sounding out the memories of the oldest among her clan to see if they ever remembered such a thing taking place.

She presented it as a matter of pure curiosity. She and Heikon had agreed to continue keeping the secret of their true connection from the clans ... for now, anyway. Neither of them wanted to dredge up the entire tragic story every time they had to explain why they could no longer do all the things mates could do, including sensing each other at a distance and being able to recognize when the other was in danger.

No, their tragedy was a private thing, and both of them continued to hold it close to their hearts. It was not for others to pull out and examine. The down side was that, without knowledge of their entire complicated backstory, both of their clans would go on viewing their affair as a temporary thing, the sort of dalliance that dragon shifters indulged in during their long lives before finding their true mates. If it felt more real, more permanent, there was nothing she could really say to convince her clan. And, with the mate bond broken, perhaps her clan would be right.

Maybe that was why she felt happier and more fulfilled

among her human friends right now than with her own clan. Humans didn't have the same expectations as shifters. They didn't know about fated mates. *All* their loves were like this one: fragile and perhaps impermanent things that had to be worked on, every day, to make them work.

And yet, they *did* make them work. Albert and Greta, over fifty years married, were still wrapped up in each other at every dance class. Lupe and George arrived at every class hand in hand; Judy and Beatrice danced as if there was nothing in the world for them except the other.

And when Esme shared her own new relationship with her human friends, their open, uncomplicated happiness for her was a balm to her soul, compared to her clan's guarded uncertainty.

And they *were* friends. She started to make a habit of meeting whichever of the ladies were available (frequently Lupe, sometimes Judy and Bea, occasionally Greta or one of the beginning students) for coffee or lunch. She stopped by the senior facility where Miriam lived, bringing fresh-baked cookies for the old people, and talked to the director about hosting a '40s dance night with her collection of big-band records.

Hardly a conversation went by without someone commenting on how happy she looked.

She *felt* happy. She felt light as a balloon. She danced through her life; she hummed as she cooked and moved from kitchen to table with little skipping dance steps. Her heart was full; her *life* was full. She had Heikon, she had her dance studio, and she had a grandchild on the way, with frequent updates from Melody, finally culminating in a visit from Melody and her mate, Gunnar.

"It's good to see both of you," Esme said, hugging first Melody and then Gunnar and then Melody again. Her daughter was very visibly pregnant now, filling out the drapery of a silky, floating maternity blouse. Their bookmobile was parked at the curb. For whatever reason—Esme couldn't fathom it, but it seemed to make Melody happy—they'd decided to take to the road with a mobile bookstore in a remodeled RV.

"And you look amazing, Mom," Melody said, standing back to hold her mother at arm's length. "I gotta say, this guy seems to be a lot better for you than Dad was."

Esme just snorted. Darius was happy with his new mate, from what she'd heard, and she'd sent a gift to their wedding—music, of course, neatly curated for wedding dancing. Beyond that, she had no particular thoughts to spare for Darius. He had his life, and she had hers, and it had been that way for a very long time—since years before she'd met Heikon.

"So you're still not going to tell Grandma if it's a boy or a girl, hmm?" she asked, as Melody reflexively put a hand on the curve of her stomach.

Melody's eyes danced. "Nope. We're keeping that part to ourselves. I can tell you one thing, though: there are two of them."

"Two ... babies? You're pregnant with twins?"

Melody nodded as Gunnar put an arm around her. "We haven't said anything because we weren't sure until my last ultrasound," she said. "I guess I had to catch up with Ben!"

Melody's half-brother Ben and his mate already had a daughter, Skye. Did they have another one now? Esme hadn't been paying much attention to that branch of the family. Ben was Darius's son by a different woman, and he'd grown up with his mother; Esme had only met him a few times.

Maybe she should make an effort to get in touch. Their children would be cousins of her own grandchildren, after all. The family, it seemed, was growing by leaps and bounds.

"Twins," she said, shaking her head. "And you still won't tell me if they're boys or girls. Or perhaps both?"

There were mutual headshakes and identical grins from Melody and her big, blond mate. "You'll just have to wait and find out when everyone else does," Melody said.

～

They had dinner with Heikon in Esme's penthouse. She was braced for ... well, she wasn't even sure what, exactly. That they'd hate each other? It was a fraught situation; Melody had a somewhat conflicted relationship with her overbearing father, and Esme wasn't sure how she was going to react to another dragon clanlord in her mother's life.

But as it turned out, everything went wonderfully. Dinner was pasta with shrimp in a butter sauce, with a side salad, and everyone chipped in to help. Melody and Heikon seemed to like each other, and Gunnar was the kind of laid-back person who got along with everyone, despite his tattooed-bruiser looks. Esme put on some music and poured wine (tea for Melody), and the dinner slipped away in a lazy haze of good food and better company.

Afterwards, they lounged around and chatted on the couch. Melody had slipped off her shoes and her mate was massaging her feet, while Heikon had his arm around Esme. Melody sat forward suddenly, nearly dislodging Gunnar.

"I just had the best idea, Mom. What do you think of a family vacation in Greece? We haven't been there in ages, and I know how much you love it. I wouldn't mind some time laying around in white beach sand myself."

"You mean just us?"

"Us, Heikon, anyone he wants to invite."

Greece. At the very mention of the word, Esme felt her

soul yearning for her sea cave, the Heart of her hoard. She could take Heikon there and show it to him. And Melody was right. It had been too long since they'd enjoyed the sun and sand of the country that she'd fallen in love with when she first visited as a young dragon.

Still ... there were considerations. "Is it safe for you to travel?"

Melody rolled her eyes. "Oh, Mother, I'm barely into the seventh month, and it's a perfectly healthy pregnancy according to my doctor. There's no reason why I can't. If it gets close to my due date while we're there, I can have the babies in Greece, or maybe we could go back to your family home in Switzerland. If anything, lounging around on the beach would be better for me than being here with all the traffic and stress, don't you think?"

Esme tipped her head back to look up at Heikon. "What do you think? Do you like Greece?"

"I've never been," Heikon said. "Unlike you, I'm not much of a world traveler."

"If you'd prefer to stay here ..." She tried not to display her heartbreak at the thought. Greece without Heikon seemed suddenly empty. Even the sea cave was no compensation.

"I didn't say that." His chest, against which she was reclining, vibrated with a low chuckle. "In fact, I might bring some of the kids. Would that be a problem? It would be a good experience for them. The youngest ones have never been away from the mountain."

Greece, here we come, Esme thought.

Her life had never been better. And yet, a cold chill crept down her spine. It was the feeling the old ladies in her dance class might describe as "a goose just walked over your grave."

The last time she'd felt this way, everything had ended in disaster.

She tried to push away the feeling away. It was going to be fine. There was no unknown danger creeping up on them.

"You okay?" Heikon murmured into her ear.

"I'm fine," she said. "Better than fine." And tried to make herself believe it.

HEIKON

Greece was very ... bright, Heikon couldn't help thinking.

It wasn't that he'd never gone anywhere at all. But his life had revolved around the Aerie for many, many years. His trips were mostly for business, and not that frequent. Usually he got his business done and went home again.

Traveling for pleasure, let alone going on vacation, was a whole new thing for him.

He stood on a patio overlooking the ocean at the island villa Esme's family had owned for over a century. All around them the Aegean Sea stretched gorgeous and blue-green, shimmering under the sun. The beach was dazzlingly white. Happy squeals drifted up to him as the kids played in the waves.

He had decided to bring Kana and the grandkids, as well as Reive for additional security. If all went well, Kana would go home in a couple of weeks, and some of the other kids and their parents would come and visit then.

"Penny for your thoughts," Esme murmured, slipping up behind him and sliding an arm around his waist.

"Shouldn't that be a drachma?"

"Wow, that's quite the unfavorable exchange rate," she bantered back. "Anyway, it's the euro now."

Heikon turned to look back down at the beach. The kids, both in their dragon forms, were splashing in the waves, diving in and out like tiny otters. The other adults watched them from the beach.

"You're not supposed to look this worried on vacation," Esme murmured, rubbing his back.

"It feels so strange to let them shift here, away from the mountain. I've spent so much time urging them to be cautious in the human world."

"But we're not really *in* the human world, no more than your mountain is. We're just a bit closer to it." She wrapped her arms around him and rested her head against his back. "My family has owned this part of the island since it was all goat herds and olive trees. It's much more touristy now, but we still have this end all to ourselves. The cliffs block the view from the town on the south end of the island. As long as we don't fly too high, we can shift here in perfect safety."

Heikon turned around to circle her in his arms. She slid into the embrace, a perfect fit, as if their bodies still recognized they were two halves of a whole, even if their shifter animals didn't. He could tell by the feel of her body that she was relaxed, in a way he'd hardly ever seen her, even at her dance studio.

If nothing else, this excursion was an opportunity to see more of her than he regularly got a chance to ... in all ways. Today she wore a pale green summer dress, sleeveless and short-skirted, with flat gold sandals and nothing else. Heikon felt positively overdressed in his light shirt and slacks.

"You love it here, don't you?" he said.

"I do." She laced her arms lazily around his neck and gave him a kiss. Even the way she moved was different here, languid and slow, as if she had all the time in the world to get where she was going. "I don't think I'd want to live here all the time. I'd miss restaurants and ballrooms and movie theaters. Cell phones. The internet." The villa was largely lacking in modern amenities, beyond a few creature comforts such as running water. Even their land line only worked intermittently. It was like the island had been caught out of time, though progress seemed to be managing to advance just fine on the other end, where the tourist hotels were.

"I'm surprised you can manage without your cooking shows."

She snorted, and kissed the tip of his nose. "It's nice to get away from it all. Even you seem more relaxed away from the mountain and all its stresses. Though you keep finding things to stress about here."

They both peered over the parapet at their families on the beach. Melody was relaxing in the shade with a book, while Gunnar hovered. Down by the water's edge, Reive had just gone to stop the kids from swimming too far out. Kana shifted into her dragon—small, slender, wingless, and powder-blue—and slipped into the water seamlessly, hardly leaving a ripple.

"They look like they're occupied," Esme said. "Can I show you something? We'll be back by lunch."

"Lead on."

She smiled and took his hand.

They went past the scattered remains of breakfast on the long outdoor table—fresh bread, pastries, fruit and olives—and on into the shadow of the house, seeming very dark after the brilliant sunshine. Heikon had done a bit of exploring on the villa's extensive grounds, but he hadn't been where Esme took him now. They went around the back of the olive groves, and Esme waved to the caretakers who were tending the villa's chicken flock at the far end. Esme had explained that the Panagapolouses were an old shifter family that her own family had employed for many years; they mainly stayed out of the way when Esme's family was in residence.

"What do they turn into, anyway?" Heikon asked as they went down a path that appeared to be leading to the sea, though it twisted around between dense stands of brush; it was hard to tell where they were going to end up.

"Dolphins," Esme said. "For the most part. I think Elena is a falcon ... or maybe Isidor? I haven't really kept up on the younger generation, to be honest. My parents would know. Oh, that reminds me." Her hand tightened on his. They walked under a bower of olive branches, trained to grow across the path; Heikon couldn't help looking up at it, filing away ideas for his own gardens back home. "You took me to meet your mother, but I haven't returned the favor."

"I know your parents already," Heikon reminded her. "Clanlord business. Not well, but I see them a few times a century."

She laughed. "And when was the last time?"

"Er ... thirty or forty years ago, it must be."

"Then I suppose we're overdue for a family lunch."

The path became steep, little more than a goat track through the brush. The ocean was visible now, and the white-sand beach, framed in the sweep of the horseshoe-shaped cliff that shut the beach and its unusual residents away from the prying eyes of the human world. They were at the top of the other wing of the cliff, across from the end of the beach with shallow water and good swimming conditions. He hadn't been up here yet.

"Now, there are two ways we could go here." Esme stood on the edge of the cliff, the ocean breeze fluttering her light dress. "The path goes on down, but it doesn't really go anywhere. It dead-ends and you have to climb over rocks. Or ..." She turned around, smiled at him, and then spread her arms and fell backwards off the cliff.

"Show-off," Heikon said affectionately, and jumped after her.

She'd shifted in midair, of course, but rather than spreading her wings to soar, she folded them and dived. Heikon was just in time to see her hit the water, arrowing into it like a diving bird of prey.

"So that's the game?" he asked, and dived after her.

The water was crystal clear, and deep enough that he didn't touch bottom even with the momentum of the dive. He twisted around, opened his eyes underwater, and looked up. Esme glided over him, a long dark shadow against the brilliance of the surface.

He'd rarely done much swimming underwater, and he'd forgotten the technique of it. His wings dragged; there was a way of folding them to gracefully glide through the water, as Esme was doing, but he couldn't seem to find it. Up there was bright and filled with sunshine, but down here in the dark—

—the dark—

Darkness and water and cold.

For months—years—he'd lain in the freezing mud at the bottom of the lake, in a coma so profound it mimicked death. His body was beyond the need for food or air. Slowly, in that darkness, in those depths, he'd healed and recovered and clawed his way back from the grave.

He didn't remember waking. He only remembered the desperate struggle for air—for light—fighting his way upward from the darkness with a body so weak it could barely move. The surface eluded him. Every time he was close, he kept slipping back.

He was drowning. He was dying—

Heikon!

Esme's voice, shocked and strong, came out of the dark, seeming to come from his mind itself. She was there, wrapping her sinuous body around him, bearing him toward the light.

He'd come back to himself enough by the time they reached the surface that he was able to swim the last few strokes on his own. Still, it was with profound relief that he broke through into the dazzling sunshine and gulped the warm Mediterranean air. He hadn't been down long enough to be truly desperate for air yet, not in this form—dragons could hold their breath a long time. But he felt starved for oxygen anyway, and cold to the bone even though the water was pleasantly warm against his scales.

"Heikon, what happened? What's wrong?"

"Bad memories." He was starting to come back to himself, feeling less shaky and cold. Esme continued to buoy him up in the water, her strong scaly back just under him and her head creasing the wavetops so she could breath. He would mind it more if he wasn't all too conscious of the dark depths of the water underneath him, too viscerally aware of the feeling of straining for air when there was none to be had.

"Something went wrong. You were in trouble." She nudged his head with her own. "Did you land badly? I'm sorry, I've spent my whole life diving off these cliffs. I forgot you were new to it."

"It's not that. Not you. It took me back, that's all."

"Back?"

"After Braun poisoned me, I fell into a mountain lake. If not for that, they'd probably have found me and killed me for real. But I woke ..." He had to stop, and take a few more breaths, reassuring himself that the air was there; it hadn't vanished.

Esme rubbed her body along his side, providing wordless comfort. "I didn't know it was still that much of a ... thing."

"Neither did I."

She went on with the caresses, her scaly side against his. "What I wanted to show you is nearby, but it's going to involve diving, and diving deep. Do you want to go back to the beach? I'm fine with that. We don't have to go there."

There was a part of him that wanted to lash back against her solicitousness. He was a dragon clanlord; he couldn't afford weakness or fear. But he didn't intend to drown in an attempt to prove how macho he was. He examined himself.

"I think I'll be fine. It was just the shock of it."

"We can swim a bit first. Get a feel for it."

He didn't like the feeling that he was being babied ... but he also didn't want to go back into the darkness at the bottom of the sea. Not quite yet. Esme flexed her body playfully and shot ahead, gliding through the water with the grace of a seal. He followed her, not quite as naturally, but starting to get the hang of it.

Esme came back and sliced through the water at his side. They rolled over, tussling playfully. It helped. He was starting to feel more himself again.

"You could tell I was in trouble."

"Well, yes, of course," she said. "You were panicking down there."

"How did you know?"

"You were crying out for help."

"Was I?" He didn't remember doing it. But then, it was a blur now; he remembered little more than disjointed impressions of darkness, cold, and panic.

True mates could tell when the other was in trouble—at least dragons could. When he'd first felt the mate bond snap into place with Esme, he'd always been aware of her presence, ready to run to her side if danger threatened.

Now he reached out, feeling for the mate bond. If she'd been able to sense him, then maybe ...

It seemed for an instant as if he could almost feel something, but it slipped away before he could get a grasp on it.

He wasn't sure if Esme had been feeling for the mate bond as he had been, but he sensed the mild disappointment underlying her words when she said, "Let's go see that thing I wanted you to see. We'll be late for lunch if we stay out here too long."

With that, she turned and swam for the cliffs, an abrupt shutdown to the conversation.

She was hurt. And upset. She'd wanted it to be there as much as he had.

Feeling obscurely as if he'd failed her somehow, and annoyed with himself for feeling that way, Heikon swam after her. He was getting better at it; with his superior size and strength, he managed to catch up by the time she reached the bottom of the cliffs. There was no beach on this part of the island, nothing but the white foam of breakers crashing into the cliffside, rolling back and crashing again. Heikon had to steadily backpedal to keep from being swept along.

"What's here?" he asked.

"A cave." There was an odd nervousness in her dragon's tone. It didn't sound like fear, more like uncertainty. Not about the task in front of her, but something else. She went on, "It's never visible from the outside, even at low tide. I found it while swimming along the shore when I was a girl. Humans will never find it, I think. They can't stay under as long as we can. But we can reach it easily. Ready?"

He wouldn't let her down. Wouldn't let himself down. "Ready."

"Just stay on my tail." She took a deep breath and submerged.

Heikon went down after her.

She was just ahead of him, wriggling steadily through the water. He followed her, wings folded to his sides, pushing along with his feet and undulating motions of his body as she was doing.

They went down and down; the water grew darker and colder. He felt a few twinges of fear, but it wasn't overwhelming, nothing he couldn't keep under control. It was true, what he'd said to her, that surprise had been the main problem before. He'd been in the water several times already, had gone swimming without giving a single thought to the mountain lake that had almost become his grave. The shock of the water closing over his head, swallowing him, was what had really done it to him. He felt better as long as he was in control.

Just up ahead, Esme angled through the rocks. The ebb and flow of the surf was weaker this far below the surface, though Heikon could feel it tugging at his body in strange ways; there were erratic currents here, unexpected undertows, the kind of thing that could easily seize a human swimmer and dash them against the rocks.

He could see why humans didn't come here.

But dragons were much bigger and stronger.

It was almost pitch dark here, now that the rock had closed around them. He felt rock scraping against his back, and more rock, crusted with barnacles, brushing his feet when he paddled. Panic ran cold fingers down his spine, but he fought it back. Esme wouldn't take him anywhere unsafe. She'd said they could get through easily. He trusted her.

And then they were in the clear again, going up. Esme broke the surface and he splashed up an instant later.

They were in a large pool, surrounded by stone. High rock walls arched above them like the interior of a dome. Surprisingly, there was light, coming down from somewhere high above. Sunlight shafted through the interior of the cave, making it look like a painting.

The cave's vast, nearly circular dome echoed back all the many tiny splashes of the water lapping around them, lending it an odd musicality. It was like being surrounded by a strange, wild symphony.

"There's an exit to the cliffs up above, but it's impossible to reach." Esme's voice echoed in the same eerily beautiful way as the wavelets splashing onshore. "It does let in light and air, though."

Wait—her voice was her human voice again. She'd shifted back; she was treading water, the skirt of her pale green dress billowing around her like a mermaid's fins.

Heikon shifted too. The water felt suddenly cooler. "What is this place, Esme?"

"Can't you guess?"

The strange acoustic properties of the cave echoed back her voice with perfect clarity. She turned and stroked toward the shore.

Heikon followed, swimming more clumsily in his slacks and shoes. He shifted back to a dragon for the last part of the swim, shifting again onshore. Esme was climbing out, wringing out handfuls of her skirt.

There wasn't much of a shore, just a strip of crumbled rock circling the pool at the heart of the sea cave. Heikon could see, on the walls, crusts of water and salt marking the height of the tides.

Esme hummed. It wasn't loud, but the walls caught and reflected it, echoing it back in a thousand overtones of harmony, as if she was humming with herself. When she stopped, it took the echoes a while to die away, as if her voice had been trapped in the cave.

As silence returned, broken only by the glassy piano-key

tinkling of the lapping waves, she turned to him. "This is the Heart of my hoard, Heikon."

"Oh," was all he could say.

He had occasionally wondered what she might have placed at the center of her hoard, the treasure beyond all treasures, but he had expected it would be a record, or a song. He had not anticipated that it would be a place.

"The acoustics in this cave are unique." The walls picked up her voice and cast it back, turning even her ordinary words into a song. "In a way, it's sort of a natural autotuning, but richer and deeper than any machine could hope to match. The first time I found it, I spent hours in here, singing to myself, leaving only when it got dark. I've never brought anyone else here. Melody knows about it, but she doesn't know where it is."

For a long moment, there was nothing he could think of to say. He had never been gifted with such an expression of trust. He didn't know how to respond.

And then he did. He began to sing.

Prior to meeting Esme, Heikon had rarely listened to music, particularly anything produced in the last hundred years, but he did like opera. He picked a duet part from one of the few operas he knew well enough to sing along with. As soon as the first words left his mouth, he felt a sting of sharp regret that he hadn't let her pick the music; what if she didn't know it?

But of course she did. After two hundred years of hoarding music, there wasn't a lot of it that Esme wasn't somewhat familiar with. Particularly an opera in her native Italian.

Heikon's bass voice thrummed through the cave. Esme's mellow alto lifted the higher notes, rising up into the soprano range once she really got going.

The music filled the cave, their voices twining together,

supporting each other. She was right; there was something magical about the cave's acoustics. It was hard to believe they didn't have a full orchestra and backup singers supporting them.

Heikon sang until he ran out of the part he was sure of and slipped into humming. Esme continued to sing for a few moments longer, until ending on a high, quavering note that seemed to linger impossibly in the cave's clear air.

For a minute or two after that, neither of them could speak. Magic, Heikon thought. It was like magic. But it wasn't. The only magic here was that of sound waves and octaves.

Esme turned to him. Her eyes, huge and bright, glistened with tears. "I've never experienced anything like that before."

"Neither have I."

She put her arms around him, and he just held her, until the clamminess of his underwear got too distracting.

"This has been one of the most amazing experiences of my life," he said. "And now what do you say to swimming out to the beach and drying off a bit?"

Esme laughed. The cave caught it, reflected it, turned it to music. "I'd love to."

She shifted and slipped back into the water. He followed. This time when she dove, he went down without hesitation, swimming without fear on her tail until they emerged into warm, clear water and sunlight once again.

It was a short swim from there to the end of the beach, where the cliffs came down to the water's edge. Around the curve of the horseshoe-shaped beach, Heikon glimpsed the rest of their family splashing in the water, too far away to make out individuals. He and Esme both shifted in the shallows, so wet by now that it made no difference, and splashed ashore and fell laughing in the warm sand.

He felt ... *young*. They rolled over and over, kissing and

laughing, with sand plastered to their wet clothing, and he felt as if the years and the centuries had fallen away. The world seemed wide-open and new, full of possibilities.

Esme rolled off him and sprawled in the sand. Her hand sought his, and their fingers entwined.

"Thank you for taking me there." He took a breath: trust shared was trust doubled. "The Heart of my hoard—"

He stopped as a shadow fell over them. They both sat up as Kana dropped to the sand, flying in the twisting way of wingless dragons. She shifted as she touched down. "There you are! I was afraid I wouldn't be able to find you."

Kana looked utterly panicked. Heikon was on his feet in an instant. "What's wrong? Is it the children?"

She shook her head, but accepted his steadying hands when he reached for her. "No. It's not that. We—" She stopped and took a steadying breath. "We just got a call at the house. They've been trying to reach us since yesterday."

"Who?" Heikon asked. All his protective instincts were already bristling.

"The Aerie. Grandfather ..." She sucked in a deep breath. Her eyes were huge. "He's back. Your brother. Uncle Braun."

ESME

By the time they got to the villa, flying as fast as possible, everyone else had gathered inside. The children were fussy and fretful, picking up on the adults' anxious mood.

"Mother," Melody said, hugging her as soon as she came in, then let go just as quickly. "You're wet!"

"I'll change in a minute," Esme said, swiping uselessly at her sodden hair. "What happened?"

"Reive heard the phone ring." Melody turned to the other young dragon.

Reive nodded. "I flew up to see what they wanted, and it was Aunt Anjelica back home. They've been calling and texting, but of course, no one's phones work out here. They finally managed to get through to the villa landline." His voice was calm enough, but he curled his hands on the edge of the table, tendons flexing in the backs. "Your mother is at the Aerie now. Great-Grandma. She was ... apparently hiding my grandfather at her den. I don't understand why she would do such a thing—"

"Because I asked her to," Heikon said.

He spoke quietly, but his voice carried through the room. Esme turned. He stood with his shoulders back, facing the others with the dignity of a dragon clanlord wrapped around him.

Somehow he managed to pull it off despite his soaked clothes and the wet hair straggling down his forehead.

Esme had never been more proud of him than she was in that moment.

"Uncle ..." Reive said helplessly. "*Why?*"

"Because I made a choice. I could have killed my brother in cold blood. I *should* have killed him, I know, for the good of the clan and for my own revenge. But I couldn't do it, and I stand by that. Instead, I took him to my mother."

"Well, something clearly went wrong." Reive's voice was tight. "Great-Grandmother said that she believes the gargoyles helped your father escape."

The gargoyles. Esme's chest tightened. The gargoyle-dragon war had raged, on and off, for untold centuries. They had wiped out Darius's clan, and she had personally fought them. The old conflict had finally been laid to rest, she'd thought, after the last battle at the Aerie. But there could easily still be factions among the gargoyles who chafed at the peace and yearned to restart the war.

And who else to feed those old hatreds but a deposed dragon clanlord with a grudge against his own clan?

Even within this room, tension was strung tighter than piano wire. Reive bristled, looking one step away from shifting and challenging Heikon.

"This decision affects the entire clan, but you made it without consulting us."

"I am your clanlord, boy." Heikon's dragon rumbled in melodic undertones to his deep voice. "I hope, for your sake, that you never have to make a decision like that. Do not second-guess me."

"You didn't tell us!"

"Do you truly fail to understand why I didn't want it getting out that I'd let my enemy live? You don't see how I'd be opening myself up to endless challenges that way? Then it's a good thing I'm in charge and you're not."

Reive growled.

"Stop!" Esme snapped. She let her dragon rise enough to snarl, until all heads turned to her. "We have bigger problems right now than each other. Braun could be anywhere in the world right now. He could be preparing an attack on the Aerie."

"He could be coming here," Kana said softly, putting her arms around her children.

Heikon set his jaw and turned to Esme. "How defensible is this place?"

"Not very," she admitted, turning to look at the wide-open archways leading out to the patio, letting in the ocean breeze. The house was designed for comfort, not for keeping out enemies. "The most defensible parts are probably downstairs, where the wine cellar and the kitchens are." She hissed softly. "Someone needs to warn the Panagapolouses. If there's fighting here, they could be targets. They should temporarily relocate to the town."

"I'll go," Melody said, heaving her heavy body out of her chair.

"Gunnar, go with her," Esme told him. He nodded and followed her out.

"The rest of you," Heikon said, "start moving food and bedding to the wine cellar. We're going to den up down there."

"This isn't over, Uncle," Reive said softly. His dragon flashed in his eyes.

"I expect not." There was both anger and resignation in

Heikon's tone. He jerked his head at Esme. "Come with me. I want to talk to you."

They both went into the master bedroom they'd been sharing. Like the rest of the villa, it was open and airy, with curtains fluttering in the windows and a huge bed covered with blankets in seafoam colors. Esme began pulling her spare clothes out of the chest at the foot of the bed. At the very least, she needed to get into something dry.

Heikon rummaged in the nightstand. "You're going to be in charge of the domestic defenses. I absolutely cannot risk Braun getting his hands on anyone he can use as a hostage. You can hole up in the wine cellar—"

He was still talking, but Esme stopped hearing it past the angry humming in her ears. She straightened up with her hands full of underwear. "You had better not be thinking about leaving me." *Again!* screamed a voice in the back of her mind. It might have been her dragon; it might only have been an echo of memory, the ghost of all those lonely nights when she'd been so lost in her grief that she could see no way forward, no future without him that wasn't endlessly long and empty.

"I don't have a choice," Heikon said. "I have to get back to the Aerie."

"Oh, and how are you planning to do that? Fly across the ocean until your dragon falls into the sea from exhaustion? Spend the next ten hours on a jet, out of touch exactly when we need you the most?"

"Well, what am I supposed to do?" he snapped. "My clan is back there. My home is back there. Braun took it from me once—"

"And this time you know he's coming! Give them instructions to batten down the mountain and wait it out. You already withstood one gargoyle siege. You can handle another."

"He could still have sympathizers inside the Aerie."

She'd forgotten about that. "So how is it better if you're there than here? What can you do there?"

"I can lead them!" Heikon roared. "I can show them I'm the lord they followed for hundreds of years! Not some hatchling huddled on a resort island across the sea."

"Protecting his mate and his family," she shot back. The word *mate* dropped out of her mouth without her conscious intention; she saw his startled look, but she couldn't call it back, so she blazed forward instead. "They need you there, but we also need you *here*. Instead of running off on your own, let's sit down and deal with this like a family. Maybe we'll all decide to wait it out here, maybe you'll take us back with us and we'll deal with things at the mountain, but the point is, Heikon—" She was shocked to find tears in her eyes. "The point is, you left me for twenty years, and you're not doing it again! Show me you've changed, and for once in your life, think things through before running off into danger by yourself again."

For a moment, he just stared at her across the bed; then he shook his head, and the defensive anger faded away. "I don't think I've ever been accused of not thinking things through," he murmured. "If anything, I've spent too much time in my life holding back and trying *not* to be an impatient whelp who flings himself into a decision without considering all sides. In a way, that's what got us into this mess in the first place."

"So take some advice once in a while." She tried to stop her voice from cracking in the middle, and didn't quite succeed.

Heikon came around the bed and took her into his arms, wet clothes and all. "As always, you offer wise counsel, my love ... my mate."

"I don't think I've ever been accused of *that*." Her voice shook. "And I'm not your mate."

"Aren't you? Are you not my love and my partner, the other half of my heart? What else is a mate but that?"

"The mate bond's still missing," she said to his chest.

"I don't know about yours," he murmured into her hair, "but my dragon's been known to be wrong once or twice. Sometimes I'm the one who has to straighten that stubborn reptile out."

Esme managed to huff out a small laugh. "Mine too, but don't let her hear you say that."

Too late, her dragon sulked. But other than that, it didn't seem to have any objections to Esme staying in Heikon's arms as long as she wanted.

All too soon, however, he let her go. "Time grows short," he said regretfully. "We must regroup in the wine cellar—and I need to give you this."

He placed something in her palm. It was cool on her skin, heavy for its size. A chain followed, coiling smoothing between her fingers.

It looked like a large gold pendant or locket. There was a complex, abstract design embossed on the front, surrounded by inlaid green stones.

"You bought me jewelry?" It did look like something she'd wear. It also looked old.

"We've had that in my family for a long time. It does look like it was made for you, though. Perhaps it was—or meant for you, at least." With a faint smile, he touched the side, and then guided her fingers to it. "The catch is here. Press like so —yes." There was a click, and the locket sprang open.

It was full of what she took at first to be small, wrinkled brown nuts. There was something vaguely familiar about them, but it wasn't until she noticed the dried flower petals nestled among them that she realized what she was looking at.

"Are these cherry seeds?"

"They're from my sakura grove." Heikon's hand closed around hers, pressing the locket shut again; she felt it snap closed as their combined fingers hid it from view. "I think you've already guessed what it is to me."

"It's your heart," she whispered. "The Heart of your hoard."

"Yes. And also no. You probably know, if you've talked to Darius about it at all, that for a long time the Heart of my hoard was kept by a human family. They were the gardeners who tended the grove."

"Tessa's family," she said quietly, thinking of Darius's cat-loving daughter-in-law.

"That's right. But, although I didn't know it at the time, it wasn't just them. It was them, and it was the trees they tended, and it was every seedling that was taken by a member of my far-flung family when they traveled, and brought back when they returned home."

His hand wrapped around hers, imprinting the smooth curve of the locket into her palm.

"Keep this for me, Esme. You must protect it, so no matter what happens to the rest of the trees, some of them will survive. Can I count on you?"

"Yes," she whispered. "I swear."

Heikon kissed her gently. Trapped between them, the locket, wrapped in their linked hands, pressed against her chest. Then he stepped back, and Esme turned so he could fasten the chain around her neck. It rested between her breasts, warmed by their hands so that she could barely feel it. The weight settled against her body as if she had been waiting all her life for it.

Heikon kissed her neck and resettled the damp mass of her hair against her skin.

"Wherever these seeds are, Esme, I'm there too, and as long as these seeds survive, I will live. Remember that."

She turned to look at him, but had no opportunity to say more, because just then, the screaming started.

It was coming from the wine cellar.

HEIKON

H eikon raced down the stairs, with Esme a step behind him, fleet on her bare, sandy feet.

At the bottom of the stairs, they found chaos.

The first thing he noticed as he charged inside was a powerful reek of wine. Whole racks of bottles had tipped over and shattered on the floor.

Both Kana and Reive had shifted, their dragons twining around each other, blue and copper, barely able to fit in the small space. Melody was pressed against the wall, trying to hold onto the children, who had both shifted and were scrabbling all over her with their little claws. There was a roar and a flash of white fur, letting him know that Gunnar had shifted as well.

In the confined space, through the heaving masses of lurching dragon scales, he couldn't even figure out what they were fighting at first. His initial confused impression was that they were fighting the walls themselves. And then he realized that he wasn't entirely wrong.

There were gargoyles in the cellar.

They were coming out of the walls, tearing themselves

free of the stone to lurch into the fight. These were even more crude and rough than the ones he'd fought at the Aerie; they looked like badly made statues, a lumpy assortment of half-carved limbs and claws and crudely made heads. None of them looked capable of independent existence. But all they had to do was attack, pounding on their opponents and ripping at them with crude claws and teeth. Reive and Kana were both bleeding, and the grinding and crashing was deafening: rock smashing into rock, claws screeching across stone.

"Upstairs!" Heikon bellowed. "Get away from the walls!"

Esme got her arms around Melody and the kids, hustling them up the stairs. There was no room for Heikon to shift with the cellar full of other dragons. "Shift back!" he shouted. "Get upstairs!"

First Kana, then Reive shifted, leaving only Gunnar's polar bear, with blood glistening on its white fur as it snarled and snapped in a frenzy. Heikon surged past his retreating clanmates, shifting as he went. The cellar was suddenly too small to contain an enraged, full-grown alpha dragon. He butted his armored head into the gargoyle attacking Gunnar, smashing it against the wall. *"Get upstairs!"* he roared at Gunnar.

The polar bear shifted to a dazed, naked human, bleeding from a dozen cuts. Heikon used one great forepaw to thrust him toward the stairs, where Reive caught him and boosted him after the others.

"They're not clever, but they're tough!" Reive yelled over the grinding and crashing of stone as more gargoyles tore loose from the walls. "Hard to fight them down here!"

"Then we won't," Heikon retorted. He reared up and pressed his powerfully muscled shoulders against the ceiling. "Get upstairs. Make sure everyone's away from whatever is above this."

Sorry, Esme, he added inwardly as the wine cellar groaned around him. But the villa could be rebuilt. People couldn't.

He withdrew hastily as the ceiling began to collapse, the walls crumbling inward. Shifting at speed, he scrambled up the stairs and staggered out onto the main floor of the villa as the walls creaked and the floor sagged. A great crack ran through the middle of the kitchen, with the floor caved in on either side.

"Sorry about your house, my love," he gasped, stumbling into Esme at the top of the stairs.

"It's only a house ... my love. We can rebuild."

"Are you all right?"

"Don't worry about me!" She gripped at his arms. "Are *you* all right?"

"I'm fine." He wiped blood from a shallow scrape on his neck. "But that won't hold them for long. Those gargoyles are smashed, but a dozen more could be made from the rubble. Where is everyone?"

"In the bedroom. I didn't know where else to go."

"It'll do for now. Come on." He caught her hand and pulled her along.

"Those were the mindless construct kind, right?" she asked, running along beside him. Around them, the villa creaked and groaned ominously. "That means there's another master gargoyle around here somewhere, right? Like the one we fought at the Aerie?"

"Yes, and he must be close."

They nearly ran into a snarling Reive at the door to the bedroom. As soon as he recognized them, he fell back and let them in. Melody was on the bed, with Gunnar bending over her. Kana guarded the door leading out to the patio.

"We've got another problem," Reive said.

"How many more problems can we have?" Heikon demanded, and then Melody let out a tortured cry.

"Oh, baby, no," Esme whispered, kneeling on the bed next to her to put her arms around her daughter. Her face hardened. "Did *they* do this? How bad is it?"

"It's not ... oh ..." Melody gasped and clutched at her pregnant belly. "It's the stress, I think. My babies ..." She looked up, in panic, into her mother's face. "They're coming now."

"We have to get out of here," Kana said from the doorway. She had one of her children wrapped around her neck, the other in her arms, both dragon-shaped.

"We can go to my cave—" Esme began, looking up with both arms wrapped around a moaning Melody.

"Your cave is made of stone!" Heikon said. As was the Aerie. And the villa. For his entire long life, caves had been safe places of retreat. He couldn't get used to thinking strategically against an enemy who could take that advantage and turn it against them.

"Water," Kana said.

"She's right!" Reive turned to Heikon. "Remember how, when the gargoyles attacked the Aerie, we took the children to the lakes? It was safe there. Well ... safer."

It still wasn't safe, Heikon thought. The gargoyles could fly. But it was better than where they were now. The rest of the house was ominously quiet, except for an occasional clatter or crash that might be something sliding off a shelf in the destabilized part of the building—or something worse.

"Stay here," he told them, and pushed past Kana, looking out into the garden sloping down toward the sea.

To all appearances, nothing had changed; nothing was wrong. It was still an idyllic Mediterranean day, the cloudless sky like an inverted blue bowl over the gleaming white sand. Shadows stood crisp as paper cutouts against the green shrubbery and white gravel paths.

But somewhere around here, there had to be at least one

master gargoyle, capable of raising stone soldiers from anything made of rock.

There had never been very many gargoyles in the world. They were rare, and slow to breed. But they had one huge advantage over the much more numerous dragons: they could augment their numbers in vast quantities with mind-less, animated statues. In the battle earlier this year, a single gargoyle named Sharpe had taken on the entire might of Heikon's clan by himself. Heikon and his people might even have lost, if not for Darius taking out Sharpe before his stone army could destroy everyone.

Heikon had never quite been sure if all gargoyles had this mastery over stone, or only some. One thing he did know was that individual gargoyles had different levels of it. Sharpe had been able to manipulate the rock of the Aerie directly, causing earthquakes and threatening to collapse the mountain's tunnels on its defenders. Heikon hadn't met another gargoyle who could do that, at least not nearly to that extent—though admittedly he had met only a few—but he'd heard of gargoyles who could phase their bodies through solid rock, or turn one kind of rock into another.

What else could *this* one do?

Frustration surged through him. He'd thought this was *over*, damn it. The gargoyles had indicated that they wanted peace. Even Darius, whose entire clan had been wiped out by gargoyles, was willing to let the old feud drop.

But somewhere, Braun had found, or had been found by, some gargoyles who shared his thirst for bloodshed and conquest.

Lucky us.

"Uh, guys," Reive reported from the other door. "More gargoyles, heading this way. They're out of the cellar and into the house."

"Hold them off," Heikon ordered. "Block the door with whatever you can find."

They scrambled to drag furniture against the door leading to the rest of the house. There were loud thumps from the other side, and a crack of stone fists striking wood. Melody let out a low cry of pain or surprise, and leaned into her mother.

"Uncle, we can't stay here," Reive said. "I don't care what's out there."

To all appearances, nothing was out there, but Heikon had never noticed just how many ornamental statues Esme had. Or had they all been there before? Were they statues at all?

The doorframe creaked, and then the door splintered near the frame and a stone-clawed fist reached through, swiping at anything in reach.

No matter how dangerous it was out there, Reive was right: they couldn't stay here.

"Up, up." Heikon helped Gunnar bundle Melody up, and then handed her off to Esme. Reive shifted abruptly, and suddenly the bedroom was full of copper and red dragon coils, sprawling everywhere. He had to; the gargoyles were breaking in, and Reive blocked them physically with his body, forcing them to fight through him to get to the others.

"Be careful!" Kana shouted, gathering the dragonlets tightly in her arms. "Grandfather, should we fly?"

"Not yet." In part because some of their number could not. Gunnar was a bear, and Melody couldn't possibly fly in her present condition. The dragons could carry the nonflyers, but their passengers would be highly vulnerable to attack. It was too dangerous. "See that gazebo? When I give the word, we'll head for that. From there, we can plan a course down to the beach."

"There's a boathouse down on the beach," Esme said. She

had one arm around Melody; Gunnar was supporting his mate from the other side. "It has a couple of skiffs in it. We can take those out."

"Good. Esme, you'll need to shift and lead us. Reive and I will cover our retreat. Keep the others in the middle. Go!"

Esme nodded. She hugged Melody and then ran forward, past Heikon, into the sunshine. For an instant as she ran onto the patio, hair gleaming in the sun, he wanted to grab her, call her back, keep her safe—

But then she shifted, and her glorious dragon, green and gold, bounded over the patio wall and into the sericulture garden of dry-climate plants beyond. "It's clear for now!" she called back. "Come on!"

Kana ran after her, carrying the dragonlets, and Gunnar followed with Melody. Heikon gave each of them a helping hand over the railing. "Reive!" he called back. He couldn't see what was happening at the door, but Reive seemed to be holding them. "Fall back. To me!"

Reive retreated, blood streaming down his lacerated neck and shoulders, but as far as Heikon could tell, the damage seemed to be superficial; he wasn't moving in the way of one who was badly hurt. Gargoyles surged after him, tearing their way through the damaged door and spilling into the bedroom.

"Go!" Heikon repeated, and he shifted on the patio. His dragon surged out of him, eager for a fight, and suddenly the railing and the open doorway into the bedroom (rapidly filling up with gargoyles) and all the human things dwindled like toys. He was enormous. He was powerful. He was—

—responsible for a woman in labor and a bunch of other noncombatants, he reminded himself.

Reive launched himself through the doorway, with the gargoyles on his heels. Heikon smashed them as they came, swatting them right and left, and then reared up on his hind legs, caught hold of the overhanging edge of the roof, and threw his entire dragon weight on it.

The roof came down in a deafening avalanche of timbers and plaster, burying the gargoyles who almost immediately began struggling to free themselves.

They were only mindless automatons, Heikon reminded himself as he brought both forepaws down on the nearest one, crushing it to gravel. Somewhere around here, their master was directing their movements. As long as that individual remained at large, he or she could create an endless army of cannon fodder.

But for now, they had a break, and he turned and half-glided, half-ran after the others. The rest of the group were most of the way to the gazebo by now, except for Reive who'd hung back to offer him backup if needed.

Which was when the garden statues attacked.

Sometimes he hated being right.

Esme's garden statues were life-sized sculptures in the old marble Greek/Roman style. Now they abruptly began to animate. A pair of fat cherubs holding a birdbath basin suddenly came to life and flapped their tiny wings, launching themselves forward to slam their basin across Reive's back. A strapping young man with his arm cocked back to hurl a spear leaped off his plinth and flung the spear; Kana rolled out of the way and it sailed harmlessly past her.

The biggest of the statues was a centaur, thundering toward them in a clatter of stone hooves. Fortunately, while horse-sized, it was still small compared to a full-grown dragon. Esme whirled around and drove its legs out from under it with a well-placed kick. Still moving forward under its own momentum, it plowed into the ground and shattered.

Heikon absently batted an erratically fluttering cherub into a decorative fountain that had not yet tried to eat anyone. Most of his attention was consumed with looking around. Whoever was doing this had to be very close in order to control the animated stoneworks so precisely. Line of sight, almost certainly. Which meant if their mysterious master gargoyle could see *them* ...

Aha!

Beyond the villa, the land rose in a rugged, rocky hillside, green with olive trees at the lower elevations, and dotted with brush higher up. In that patchwork of orange rocks and green trees, shadows and dazzling sunlight, one of the shadows moved.

There were wild goats up here, but that sure didn't look like a goat. Heikon snarled and beat down with his wings, taking to the air.

"Where are you going?" Esme shouted after him.

"To take care of our problem, I hope!"

He swept over the villa, feeling another pang for what he'd done to Esme's nice house; he'd have to make it up to her later. The gargoyle on the hill saw him, and rather than ducking to hide, beat his wings and flew up to meet him in the air.

Like all transformed gargoyles, he looked like a living statue. He was very spiky, this one, with sharp-looking spines on his shoulders and a row of them marching all the way down his arms to his wrists. Otherwise, though, he didn't really look like much. Even bulked out as a gargoyle, he wasn't especially large. If not for the complication of the stone skin, Heikon felt that he could very easily take him in a one-on-one fight. And the stone was as much of a liability as a benefit for gargoyles when they were fighting a dragon. It meant they couldn't be bitten or easily hurt, but they were vulnerable in other ways—to shattering, say. All he had to do was swat the bastard out of the air.

Heikon dived at him. The gargoyle folded his wings and twisted to the side. His small size was working for him, making him more maneuverable. It took Heikon longer to turn.

Still, Heikon was a creature of the air, born and bred to it. No gargoyle could evade him in the skies for long.

"Who are you?" Heikon demanded. "What is your quarrel with us?"

The gargoyle grinned, displaying thick fangs jutting out from his lower jaw. "I'm a forward-thinking individual," he said, his voice slurred by the fangs. "I know you think of my kind as the aggressors, but most of us just want to stay out of you dragons' way, believe it or not. Me, though—I can pick a winning side when one comes along."

"My brother, you mean? How long have you been working with him?"

"Off and on since the old days. Where do you think he got the dragonsbane he used to poison you?"

Heikon roared and charged at him. The gargoyle rolled out of the way, dropping lower in the sky.

He's making us angry on purpose, Heikon thought, directing it at his furious dragon as much as to himself. Angry people got sloppy. They made mistakes.

But as long as he could keep the gargoyle's attention on him, the more time the rest of his family—and Esme—would have to escape.

"How much dragonsbane do you have?" he demanded, beating his wings and rising to face the gargoyle once more. An army of gargoyles, armed with a drug that could immobilize and poison his kind ... it didn't bear thinking about. They could put it in the Aerie's water supply, poison the soil where they grew their food ...

"Poisons are my specialty," the gargoyle said. He glanced down at his arm, flexed his spikes. "You can call me Trenn. Though you won't be calling anyone anything for very long."

With that, he snapped his arm forward, and the spikes detached, hurtling through the air.

Heikon, shocked, started to twist away, but he could see he wasn't going to be fast enough. Then a weight impacted him from the side, knocking him toward the ground.

He got straightened out and unwound from the other dragon tangled up with him. It was Reive.

"What are you doing here?!"

Reive's dragon's jaws parted in a fierce grin. "Esme told me to come help you. I'd rather argue with you than her any day."

"Impudent hatchling."

Reive turned serious. "She also needs you to know there's another dragon incoming."

Braun. It had to be.

"What's the matter?" Heikon asked Trenn. "Did you spring your little attack too early?"

Trenn only grinned. He was keeping his distance from the two dragons. The spikes on his arm had regrown. "My job is to keep you busy. Working, isn't it?"

"Uncle ..."

There was something off in Reive's mental voice. Something strange. Heikon turned in midair, and noticed the row of gray stone spikes bristling from Reive's shoulder and arm like porcupine quills.

Reive had not just knocked Heikon out of the way; he'd taken the brunt of the attack. Now he was wobbling in the air, his wings flapping in an uncoordinated way.

A wound like that wouldn't make a difference to him normally. There's something in those spikes.

"You!" Heikon roared.

He charged Trenn, sweeping down on him in a fury. Trenn launched another wave of spikes, but this time Heikon was prepared. He ducked underneath and the spikes passed harmlessly over his head. Heikon managed to score a glancing blow on his enemy with his claws, raking across the gargoyle's stone skin. As he continued his dive past Trenn and turned in midair, his forepaw burned painfully.

The gargoyle was poison. Everything about him was poison. The spikes, maybe even his skin.

Reive was sinking groundward now, losing altitude.

And then suddenly Esme was there, soaring in at Heikon's side, green and gold and magnificent. She carried in her claws the remains of one of the shattered statues, a great hunk of stone that she hurled at Trenn.

Trenn dodged, but his confidence was clearly shaken. He began to retreat.

"Don't let him touch you; he's poison!"

"Yes, I figured that out!" she retorted. "Get something to attack him with."

Heikon dived and uprooted an olive tree. Esme had hold of a small boulder now. Between the two of them, they drove Trenn back. Every time he tried to escape, one of them was there, blocking his retreat. It was plain from the look on his face that he was starting to figure out he'd made a mistake.

"Keep him busy while I get above him," Esme said.

Easier said than done, at least without taking a load of spikes and ending up like Reive. Heikon swiped at Trenn with the olive tree, forcing the gargoyle to fly lower until his clawed stone feet brushed the ground.

And then Esme's boulder came out of nowhere and flattened him.

"Uh ... wow." Heikon dropped the tree and flew up to join her. "Remind me not to anger you, my love." His forepaw still stung viciously where he'd poisoned it on Trenn's skin; he flexed it as the burning began to fade.

"Where's Reive?" Esme asked sharply.

They found him on the ground, human-shaped once

again. His arm dangled limply, blood running down his fingers. In his human form, the spikes were much larger, protruding from his arm like knives. He was trying to remove one, fumbling at it with his other hand.

"Don't touch that," Heikon ordered, batting his hand away. "It's poison. Everything on him is poison."

"I know!" Reive retorted. His face was ashen under the bronze of his skin. "It's burning—feels like my arm is on fire."

He swayed. Esme caught him. As she did, a shadow fell across them, and a sudden wind sent dust swirling away from them in all directions.

Heikon knew what he was going to see before he looked up.

Braun hovered above them, beating his wings hard to stay in place. The downdraft blew their hair and flung dust in their faces, like the wind from a helicopter's rotors.

Heikon had seen his brother in the cave plenty of times, unconscious and out of trouble. But seeing Braun out and awake in his shift form made him realize that he'd forgotten how big Braun was. He was huge, probably the biggest dragon Heikon had ever seen. His black and green scales gleamed in the sun.

Reive struggled to stand upright. "I can still fight," he gritted out.

"I think this fight is mine," Heikon said, looking up at Braun. "Esme, get Reive and everyone else down to that boathouse you talked about. We don't know for sure that there won't be more gargoyles."

"What about you?"

She stood with her arms around Reive, holding him up as his legs sagged under him. Her sunfire hair was whipping in the wind, her face smudged with dust. She'd never had a chance to change out of her wet dress from earlier, and it had dried into a rumpled mess around her, stained now with Reive's blood.

She was the most beautiful woman in the world. His locket glistened at her throat.

"This is a fight that's been coming for twenty years," Heikon told her, and he shifted. Esme and Reive seemed to shrink as his dragon reared above them. He spread his wings, sheltering them from the downdraft of Braun's heavy wingbeats.

"And I'm not going to lose," he added, and launched himself into the air to meet his brother.

HEIKON

"Heikon."

Braun's resonant voice was the same as it had always been, familiar since childhood. They'd been close, once. It was for the sake of that long-ago bond that Heikon had let him live, unable to bear the death of the younger brother who had once followed him everywhere. He had taught Braun to fly. Together they had explored the mountains, gotten into mischief, driven their mom crazy.

And then we grew up.

He rose to Braun's level, surprised by the lack of attack, but then Braun trumpeted out in a ringing voice that must have been heard by everyone for miles around: "Heikon, I challenge you for leadership of the clan."

"Well, it's about damn time," Heikon shot back. After all of this, an ordinary challenge was a relief. The duels weren't common anymore, but they had been a well accepted way of settling disputes once.

A challenge. This he could deal with.

"Be careful, my love." It was Esme's dragon's fluting voice.

He looked down and saw that she'd shifted and gotten Reive onto her back. "You don't know he won't try to cheat."

Everything in Heikon cried out against the accusation. A duel was a matter of honor. Even Braun wouldn't violate that!

But then he looked across the space between them at Braun hovering against the sky, great black and green wings beating heavily. Braun had tried to take control of the clan by gathering a cabal against him and then trying to murder him. Of course he'd cheat, if he got the chance.

The only reason he was willing to risk a duel at all was because he no longer had the support in the clan that he once had. If he won a duel and gained the clanlordship fairly, or at least appeared to, they would have to accept him.

"We will need observers to ensure fairness," Heikon told Braun.

"Stalling! Delays!"

"You attacked my family," Heikon retorted. "I am well within my rights to demand this. You can have observers too if you like."

"I need none," Braun replied loftily.

"Esme, my love, I hate to ask this of you ..." He would rather have almost anyone else, in truth, because he did not want her to have to watch. But there was no one else available, and no one he trusted as he did her.

"Of course," she called back. "Let me get Reive comfortable. How about the beach?"

"The beach sounds perfect."

"Your 'observers' had better not intervene on your behalf, Heikon," Braun told him.

"What do you take me for?! I, unlike you, am not a cheater."

They flew down to the beach and landed on the white

sand. Hard to believe that not so long ago, the family had been enjoying themselves here in the surf and the sun.

Heikon looked around and saw Esme glide down to land nearby.

"How's Reive?" he called.

She settled herself on the sand, remaining in her dragon form, her wings half-mantled above her. "It's hard to say. Kana is taking care of him. Now that the gargoyles are no longer a threat, Gunnar has gone in search of medical help for him and Melody."

The reminder of Melody stabbed him with guilt. Of course Esme would rather be with her pregnant daughter at this important moment.

"Yes, but I also want to be with you," she said, as if reading his mind. "Melody is in good hands. Gunnar will fetch the Panagapolouses, who have lived on this island for generations. They will be able to bring a shifter doctor or midwife."

Braun rustled his wings impatiently. "Enough of these delays. Get on with it!"

"You are entitled to observers as well," Heikon told him politely.

"I need none! I don't need an audience to watch me tear you to shreds."

What this told Heikon was that Braun had no more allies. He'd been helped out by a lone, disaffected gargoyle, and that was it. Even if Braun won here today, he might still lose. He would have to stand against the clan and convince them that he was their leader by right. Heikon had a feeling that he'd be going up against formidable resistance, from Anjelica and their mom in particular. Not to mention Esme.

But we won't let him win, Heikon's dragon announced with rock-solid certainty.

Heikon opened his jaws and roared out his challenge. Braun answered it. As one, they launched from the sand and swept toward each other, clashing together in a great flurry of wings and flying claws.

It had been a very long time since he'd been in a real fight against an equally matched opponent. He felt searing pain as Braun's claws ripped through the delicate membrane of his wing. But he scored a hit too, raking his teeth down Braun's neck. They broke apart and circled each other, panting, leaving blood in the white sand.

Braun had been overconfident too, Heikon thought. Now they were both much more cautious. Around and around they went, jockeying for an angle.

He wished Esme wasn't here. He kept wanting to look over at her, even knowing he didn't dare take his attention from the battle for an instant. Anyway, Esme would be the first to tell him to keep his eyes on his business. He could almost hear her in his head, scolding him, and he found himself smiling.

"What are you smiling about?" Braun demanded.

"Just thinking about what I'm fighting for," he replied. "It's why I'm going to win, because I have something to fight for and you don't."

Braun roared and lunged, driven from his caution by fury. His onslaught drove Heikon back, and for a moment the entire world vanished in snapping jaws, slashing claws, and the necessity of throwing every atom of his attention into blocking Braun's charge before his brother's teeth could sink into his neck. Anger often bred carelessness, but in Braun's onslaught of vicious fury, Heikon couldn't find an edge. He ended up striking out with his wings, beating his way off from the sand in an attempt to gain some altitude and get an advantage.

"Running away, huh?" Braun accused, flapping heavily after him. "I might have known you'd be a coward once you started losing!"

"Losing, am I?"

Heikon dove at him, slamming into him. They twisted and struggled in midair, spinning around and around. Braun's teeth were latched into his shoulder agonizingly, but Heikon got his own jaws on one of Braun's wings. He twisted, and Braun's wing snapped.

Braun let go with a scream. Still tangled together, they both flew in a wobbly, downward trajectory and crashed into the rocky ground on the clifftops above the beach. Heikon let go and they both tumbled end over end before picking themselves up.

Braun looked bad. One of his wings trailed in the dust and he was holding up a foreleg, trying not to put weight on it. But Heikon knew he didn't look any better. Blood kept dripping in his eyes, and there was a ringing in his ears; he'd hit his head when they fell. Whenever he moved he could feel hot blood trickling from the wounds that Braun had torn open in his scaly hide.

"It doesn't have to be like this," he said as they limped around each other. Braun's head was held low and flat, bloody fangs displayed, like a vicious dog looking for a chance to bite. "Come back to me, brother. We could be allies again."

"The only thing I want from you is your death!"

Braun lunged, but the dragging wing threw him off. He clawed Heikon down the side, but Heikon got a good slash in at his other wing, and now that one was dragging too.

Braun was losing. And Heikon could see that realization dawning in his eyes.

"Don't make me do this, Braun."

"I will not lose to you!"

Another feint; another lunge. They were both panting; the rocks were splattered with blood. But Heikon felt a surge of renewed energy, even with blood running into his eyes and his entire body a mass of hurt. He was going to win, one way or another.

"You're losing, Braun. Surrender to me. We'll work something out."

"I'd rather die," Braun snarled, and he backed a couple of steps away and worked his jaws, opening and closing his mouth.

Heikon stared at him. He had no idea what Braun was doing. And then he figured it out. There was something hidden in Braun's mouth, tucked into his cheek.

Taking things with you through a shift was hard— normally everything you carried would be tucked away along with your clothes until you shifted back—but you could do it. Anything carried or worn on Braun's person would have been easily spotted during the fight. But not something hidden in his mouth.

But what *was* it?

And then the smell hit him, along with the incredibly careful way Braun was holding it on his tongue.

There was a packet of essence of dragonsbane in his mouth, the concentrated poison that would kill what it touched.

Braun's energy was clearly flagging, but he had enough for one last charge. With a tremendous effort, he lifted his broken wings, mantled them over his back, and charged.

Heikon realized instantly that if Braun managed to score a hit on him this time, he would die. They would both probably die, but apparently Braun was willing to risk it. Even a graze might do it. Dodging was too risky.

So instead, Heikon went straight into the charge. Braun clearly was not expecting that. As Braun dove in for the kill, Heikon ducked his head under Braun's chin and then snapped it up.

He was only trying to deflect Braun, but Braun's teeth

snapped together and the smell of the poison was suddenly eye-searingly intense.

But Heikon had also exposed his own soft throat, the underside of his chest. Braun lashed out with his great claws in a final spasm and tore through Heikon's neck, ripping open his throat.

Heikon fell to the ground, wheezing. His mouth filled with blood. He couldn't breathe.

Through dimming vision, he saw Braun, near him, shudder once and then lie still, a victim of his own treachery.

But Heikon was starting to realize that his own victory had come too late. He'd lost too much blood, and as he lay struggling for air, the world began to close in on him, darkness flooding to blot out everything.

The last thing he sensed was the frantic touch of Esme's mind on his. And then she was gone too, along with everything else.

ESME

Heikon!
She had followed them up to the top of the cliffs and now she flew to him, shifting as she touched down. She spared barely a glance for Braun's body, all her attention on Heikon and the blood surrounding him, covering him.

"Heikon," she begged. "Heikon!"

She dropped to her knees beside him, groping desperately under his jaw for a pulse. She couldn't feel anything. His eyes were half open. He didn't seem to be breathing.

Had he taken any of the dragonsbane? Enough to poison him? Enough to kill him? She couldn't tell.

"Heikon," she sobbed.

How could her happy future be dangled in front of her, only to be snatched away?

"Heikon!"

She bowed her head against his neck, heedless of the blood soaking into her dress and her long hair, and then she felt something fall forward and click lightly against his scales.

The necklace he'd given her.

Wherever these seeds are, Esme, I'm there too, and as long as these seeds survive, I will live.

Could he possibly mean ...?

The Heart of a dragon's hoard was not normally that powerful. But Heikon's hoard was special. It was made up of green growing things. And he'd already appeared to die and then come back once, like a tree in the winter. She had thought Braun looked dead once before, too. Things were not always what they appeared.

With shaking, blood-sticky hands, she cracked open the locket. The seeds fell into her hands. She didn't know what to do with them, but they seemed warm to the touch, perhaps only from her skin.

It was a miracle she was groping after, but right now, that was the only hope she had. The only hope *he* had.

"Heikon," she whispered. Seeds went in the ground, didn't they? She pressed the seeds into the earth under him, watered with his blood. Two of them she kept back.

"I hope this helps, my love," she whispered shakily. "I don't know what I'm doing."

She pushed one of them into his mouth, between the half-open jaws, past the still tongue. She held the other for a moment, and then quickly swallowed it.

It wasn't much fun, swallowing a cherry stone. She felt it go down in a hard lump.

Then she waited, trembling. Was she supposed to do more? Tears flooded her eyes. She had *tried*.

"I don't know what else to do," she wailed.

And then there was ... something. A change.

It wasn't in Heikon. He still didn't move, didn't breathe. It was in *her*. Something tickling the back of her mind, something she hadn't felt in a very long time.

She pushed at it, clawed at it.

The mate bond.

It was still there. Or maybe it was there again, a bond *they* had made, born from love and quickened with Heikon's blood and her own renewed grief.

The Heart couldn't bring a dragon back if they had already died. But the mate bond sometimes could. Or, at least, if Heikon was still alive, even a little bit, it was possible for one mate to support the other's faltering strength using their own. And if she could feel the mate bond, then he wasn't dead. Not quite. Not yet.

Here was her miracle, at her fingertips.

She reached for it with everything in her, poured herself into it. *Help me!* she cried at her dragon, and felt it clawing with her, lending its strength to hers.

And suddenly she felt that corridor spring wide open. Everything that had once been there was there again.

She could *feel* him. Feel his faltering heartbeat, feel the weak stirrings of his breath. Feel his love for her, underneath it all.

Our mate! her dragon cried, its inner voice torn by shock and grief. *Our mate is here. Our mate is dying!*

No! she thought back. *We won't allow it!*

"Heikon," she gasped, and she laid her hands on him, and her head on him, and she put everything she had, all her strength, all her love, into keeping him there, holding him with her so he couldn't slip away before help got there.

"I'm not going to let you go," she sobbed into his scaly skin. Her dragon was with her; they were, at last, fully united in their sense of purpose. "I let you go once. Not again. Not ever again."

Very dimly, she was aware of footsteps, of other people around her, but she didn't become aware of her surroundings again until hands were on her, trying to pull her away.

"No!" she cried, pushing back.

"Esme," said a voice, and Esme looked up, unable to believe for a moment that they were here.

Her parents?

"Esme," her mother said again, kneeling beside her. Shocked, she looked around. Kana was there too, and a couple of the Panagapolous family, all of them looking very short and out of place among the tall, red-haired Lavignas. She hadn't seen this much of her clan together in one place in years.

"What are you doing here?" she managed to get out as her clan's healers descended on Heikon.

"Your boyfriend's clan called us," her mother said, going to one knee beside her. "They'd been trying to reach you, couldn't get through, and worried that you might need some help. And we were, after all, not *that* far away. Not across an ocean, at any rate."

"And you're here," she said dizzily. With great reluctance, she allowed herself to be drawn away from Heikon, her fingers trailing across his scales. "Will he be all right, Mother?"

"No one can say for certain, dear heart." Her mother was cool and reserved as always, but she put an arm around Esme without seeming to care for the blood soaking her clothes. "But we have the very best physicians. And we arrived for the last of the fight, so we saw how strong he is. We will care for your boyfriend as if he were one of our own."

"Boyfriend ..." No. That word was wrong. Far too shallow, too crass. "Mate. He's my mate."

"Oh." It came out on a breath. "Well. No effort or cost shall be spared, then. If it is possible for him to live, daughter, then he will live."

Esme turned her face into her mother's neck, inhaling the smell of the perfume that had always meant childhood to her.

And knowing he was in good hands, knowing he would never be farther away than the mate bond, she relaxed into her mother's arms and let someone else carry the load for a while.

HEIKON

Heikon dragged himself slowly out of sleep. He had the foggy sense that he'd been asleep for some time. He felt heavy, as if his body was a weight trying to drag him back down. He struggled through it, waking further, and became aware that there were bandages on his throat and chest and ... basically everywhere, actually.

Heikon?

Esme's presence was so warm and immediate, her voice so near, that he turned his head to the side, expecting to find her with him in the bed. She wasn't, but he could still feel her, and that was when he realized why.

The mate bond?

It's back, Esme confirmed.

The door opened and she came in, skimming across the floor with her light dancer's grace. Her hair was braided down her back, and she was dressed for slightly cooler weather, in a long green skirt and a matching shirt with a row of tiny buttons up the front that almost begged to be undone.

He didn't recall that outfit in her luggage, and in fact,

looking around, he didn't think he'd ever seen this room in his life. The bed was an enormous antique with a white bedspread. Everything in the room was dark polished wood with white and gold accessories—understated, tasteful, and expensive-looking. The window was open, with lacy white curtains fluttering in a cool breeze. The scents that drifted in were lush and wild, grass and pine trees and, unexpectedly, cows. This definitely wasn't the villa in Greece.

Esme sat on the bed beside him and brushed her hand through his hair.

"Where are we?" he asked weakly.

"We're at my clan's home. Switzerland. We brought you back here after you were hurt."

Things were falling back into place, one fragment at a time. "Braun is dead, isn't he?"

"He's dead," she confirmed. "Definitely, undoubtedly dead this time. He tried to kill you by treachery and ended up killing himself instead." The corner of her mouth twisted, not a smile, more like a fierce grimace. It was an expression that was more suited to a dragon's features than a human's. "A poetic end for one who lived by treachery. I *am* sorry, though. I know he was family."

"I did nothing I regret." He rested his head against her leg, and she continued to smoothly stroke his hair. He felt that he could lie here forever. "The mate bond. It's back. How?"

"I don't know," Esme admitted. "Neither do our healers. It may have had something to do with the Heart of your hoard." She reached for the smooth skin above the bodice of her dress, and noticed him following the movement with his gaze, but her hand touched only bare skin. "I still have the necklace you gave me, but it's being cleaned. It got a bit ... er, bloody. I planted the seeds you gave me—but I'm really not sure if it had anything to do with that. It might be that we simply made the bond ourselves, through love and devotion."

She leaned her head against the bed's ornate headboard. "Who knows how it works? We already knew we were right for each other. It was just a matter of getting our animals to agree."

Mate, Heikon's dragon sighed.

You certainly spent long enough telling me that she wasn't, you stubborn reptile.

His dragon didn't reply, merely curled up in rapturous peace.

"But I haven't told you my biggest news yet," Esme said, her fingers running through his hair over and over. "Melody had her babies!"

Heikon raised an eyebrow, the only part of his body he felt like moving at the moment, and probably the only part that didn't hurt. "Babies, plural?"

"Yes, she had twins. A boy and a girl. I knew about the twins part, but what I didn't know was that those sneaks had names already picked out."

Another eyebrow raise.

"Dashiell and Daria. Dashiell is a good literary name, and I can even forgive naming her daughter after Darius, of all people." Her face was suffused with wonder. "I'm a grand-mother, Heikon."

"And a young and beautiful one you are, too."

"Flattery," she murmured, "will get you everywhere." She leaned down to kiss him. It lingered, her lips sipping at his. When she broke away, she said, "The gargoyles have sent apologies for Trenn, by the way. I don't know if I believe them or not, but they claim he was a rogue, working without the support of his ... what did they call it? His alliance. I think that's their equivalent of our clans."

"Good for them." He really didn't care. The important thing was that his clan was all right. Or were they? "Have you heard from the Aerie? Is everyone—"

"Everyone is fine. It's you we've been worried about. You've been out for three days." She snuggled down beside him, curling up against him.

"Reive?" he asked, remembering his last sight of the young dragon, half conscious on Esme's back and poisoned by gargoyle venom.

"He's recovering. The clan healers have never seen anything like it, but getting the poison spikes out seemed to stop it, and now it's just a matter of letting his body heal on its own. He's in the room next door, and he's been asking about you. I'm sure he'll be in to see you soon."

"Not sure if I'm up to visitors yet," he murmured.

"Heikon Corcoran, admitting you aren't a hundred percent well? I'm shocked."

"Maybe I just enjoy having you all to myself." He twined his fingers lightly through the strands of her braid. The mate bond between them hummed with perfect satisfaction, perfect contentment.

～

He slept again, and afterwards, he washed and ate, and dressed in borrowed clothes, a dark brown shirt and casual tan slacks belonging to Esme's father. He saw her parents briefly, offered his sincere thanks for their help and a promise of permanent friendship with his clan. Then he and Esme went walking on her clan grounds below the chalet.

He was still slow and easily tired, but he could feel himself getting stronger. The exercise seemed to be helping.

Esme's family, it appeared, went in more for interior decorating than landscaping. For the most part, the sloping hillside around the chalet was left natural, except for some groves of fruit trees and green pastures where cows grazed.

The low, deep tones of their cowbells rang across the hillside like strange music, and it occurred to him to wonder if that was what it all went back to for Esme, the melodious sound of the cowbells lulling her to sleep in her cradle.

They sat on a rocky outcropping looking down into the valley, where there was a small village below. The wind was cool and fresh, tugging loose strands of hair out of Esme's braid. The village looked like a calendar picture from up here, tiny picturesque houses with a mountain stream running through the middle of it.

"They know about dragons down there," Esme said, indicating the village. "Rather like Darius's village, where the people living there are mostly humans, but they keep his secret because it's in their best interests to do so. Back in a much earlier time, my family ruled them as the local nobility. We had a beneficial arrangement with them; we kept raiders out, and they kept our secret. These days I think it's just come to be how things are. They don't post videos of dragons on Youtube, and they enjoy a prosperous little town supported by dragon clan money."

Heikon laughed quietly.

"Something's funny?" she said sharply, looking at him.

"Not that kind of funny. Not really." He wrapped his hand around hers, chafing the backs of her fingers. "It's just that I can hear your love for this place when you talk about it. I keep thinking I've seen all the sides to you, and then I find another. The dragon princess of the cities, who loves the city lights and cultural opportunities and bustle. The world traveler who loves the Greek islands, serene and beautiful under the sun. The wild child of the mountains, who loves this small town where she grew up."

Esme snorted, but she let him keep holding her hand. "Well, it would be boring if I only enjoyed one thing, wouldn't it? As long as you don't start thinking any of those sides of me are the only side."

"I would never dream of it," he promised, kissing her fingers. "I hope you'll keep showing me all the different things you love, so that I can learn to love them too."

"Hmm." She stood, and offered him a hand up. "I'm thinking I might offer you a ride back. It was an easy walk down, but it's going to be a steep climb up, and you'll be able to see more of the view that way."

"Lead on, my love."

Her body flowed and shifted, and the dragon reared above him. Her green, he noticed now, was exactly the green of the trees behind her, and the gold patterns on her scales made him think of sunlight on meadow grass. This place suited her.

But then, so did the city, where she fit so seamlessly into the bustle of pedestrians on sidewalks, and readily adapted to new technology. So did the Greek islands, where her cave lay secret and hidden.

Some people were made to stay in one place their entire lives, and loved it that way. And some people were made to travel. Esme was one of those.

But even world travelers needed somewhere to come home to. He hoped she would come to think of his mountain as fondly as she thought of the mountains of her youth.

He thought there was a very excellent likelihood that she would.

Back at the chalet, Esme went off to see her family about dinner plans, but Heikon opted to stay outside, examining the flowers around the chalet's terraced stone patios. They didn't have a vast amount of landscaping, but what they had was understated and well planned to suit the natural curves of the land. Heikon was always eager to learn new techniques that he could apply to his gardens back home. He definitely would need to talk to their gardener.

The soft tap of footsteps on stone tiles alerted him to the presence of another person, before Reive came into view.

"Uncle," Reive said with a brief smile. He was gray and weak-looking, with his right arm swathed in bandages from shoulder to fingers. "They told me you were up and about."

"It seems that I'm recovering faster than you are," Heikon said, frowning at him. "I thought a swift recovery was the province of the young."

"*You* try taking a dose of gargoyle venom and see how you like it." Reive grimaced and sat down on a stone bench next to a bank of latticed roses. Heikon joined him; sitting down wasn't a bad idea, now that he thought about it. No sense in overdoing it.

"Esme says the gargoyles have reported that it was the action of a rogue," Heikon said.

"Wouldn't you be?" Reive said. "If this was a power play of theirs, it didn't work." He frowned, and carefully flexed the fingers of his right hand, protruding from the bandages. "Don't look at me like that. I'm getting better. And they're gargoyles; what do you expect? They're not like us."

In all honesty, Heikon had his doubts about that. From what he'd seen, the gargoyles were more similar to his own kind than not, just as he was starting to realize, from getting to know Esme's old people, that humans were not really that different from shifters after all. They all loved and grieved; they all could be generous and kind, selfish and petty. They were all people, under the skin, scales, or stone.

.... did gargoyles have fated mates? It was something he

had never really wondered about before. Perhaps they shared that too.

But now was not the time for his musings on this, not with Reive looking pale and weak from a near-fatal encounter with one of them.

"Aside from all of that," Reive said, and his face lit up with a bright grin, making him look less tired and wan. "What's this I hear about Esme being your mate? When exactly were you planning to tell the rest of us?"

"We didn't know either," Heikon protested, aware as the words came out that it didn't sound like much of a defense.

"How can you *not know*?"

"Nephew, settle in," Heikon said. He took a deep breath. "Let me tell you the story of something that started twenty years ago, and only came full circle a few days ago."

He had a feeling he was going to be telling this story a lot in the next couple of weeks. Esme had surely had similar experiences filling in her own family. But it was, at last, a story that *had* an ending—and a happy one, at that. The mate bond was a gentle presence inside his chest, a warm awareness of Esme elsewhere in the chalet—a reminder that no matter how far they were from each other, neither of them would ever be lonely, not ever again.

"It happened," he began, "at the Aerie, twenty years ago."

ESME

There was a picture on her phone, from half a world away. *I felt you should see this.*

The picture showed sun-drenched rocks. It could have been anywhere, but she recognized the brilliant sunlight and stark shadows of the Greek islands. There was still some blood visible on the rocks, dried to a rime of dark brown.

And a tiny green seedling curling up from the sandy soil.

I don't know if cherry trees will grow in the Mediterranean islands, Heikon texted. *It's entirely the wrong climate. But I guess we'll see.*

She smiled, and texted back, *We've beaten the odds before.*

I love you, Heikon texted. *I miss you.*

YOU'RE the one who decided you needed to go to Greece two weeks before your own wedding and see how the repairs to the villa were coming along.

What can I say? he texted back, and she could almost hear the wry humor behind the words. *You're the one who introduced me to the joys of world travel. You have no one to blame but yourself.*

You'd better bring me back something nice. She touched the locket at her throat. Meticulously cleaned, with fresh seeds inside, it was always with her, carrying a little of Heikon close to her heart.

I'm sure you'd never let me hear the end of it if I didn't.

Too right. And now you're going to make me late to my own class.

We can't have that, he texted. *Talk to you later, my love.*

And you, she wrote back. *My love.*

With her heart as light as the trip of her feet in her dancing shoes, she went downstairs to prepare for her last class before she left for Heikon's mountain and an indefinite stay there.

She would have loved to invite her students to the wedding, but she knew she couldn't. Even if it hadn't been held at a private dragon mountain in the middle of nowhere, there were sure to be transformed dragonlets running around under the adults' feet throughout the festivities. No matter how often they were cautioned not to shift, someone would surely slip up.

And anyway, a wedding was supposed to be a fun event. Having everyone on their best behavior, trying to hide their true selves because there were a bunch of humans underfoot, would make the entire event fun for no one.

Anyway, did she really want to explain to everyone that her fiancé owned his own mountain? No, she did not.

So she let them throw her a bridal shower instead.

She was well aware there were plans afoot. No matter how they tried to hide it, they simply were not very subtle; all the whispering would have been a dead giveaway even if she hadn't had extra-sharp dragon hearing.

But she was still surprised by her own reaction when they came in on this very last dance night, laden with packages. Everyone had brought gifts, and there were bags of decorations that Lupe and Judy immediately threw themselves into putting up. And the cake was amazing. It was several layers tall, made to look like one of Esme's green dancing dresses, complete with a realistic ruffled skirt. The top read *Congratulations and best wishes to Esme from her students* in looping handwriting.

Esme blinked hard to stop herself from inappropriately bursting into tears unbefitting a 200-year-old dragon. She had already done plenty of joy-crying over her new grandbabies; she was turning into a regular sap. "Did all of you *make* this?" she asked, leaning close to admire the piped icing folds of the skirt.

"Greta did," Bea said.

Greta blushed. "I used to decorate cakes professionally," she admitted. "I haven't made a cake like this in years. It was fun to put my hand in again."

And then the gifts were opened—all standard bridal-shower kinds of things, at least from what Esme gathered from TV and movies, never having had one herself; there were appliances she knew she'd never use, risqué lingerie (in gold and green, and surprisingly well-sized for her) that she probably would, and an ornate crystal cake server that made Greta exclaim, "Miriam! That's the one I gave you at your wedding to Herbert!" She paused. "Or was it Benjamin? Anyway, you can't regift a wedding gift!"

"It is not," Miriam said without a trace of either shame or doubt.

"It is *so*."

"Well, it's lovely, anyway," Esme said, and went to cut the cake.

Later, as cake was consumed and people broke up into conversational groups, Miriam beckoned Esme. "Dear, could I talk to you privately for a minute? If you'd just push my chair—"

Esme wheeled her into the adjacent room with the stereo equipment. The door was normally left open during dance classes so she could easily come and go, but she pulled it shut.

"And those?" Miriam said, indicating the blinds across the large window looking into the ballroom.

Esme drew the blinds as well. "When you said private, you meant private," she said, smiling, and inwardly bracing against whatever wedding-night advice was inevitably going to follow.

"I just needed to show you something," Miriam said. Her hands trembling with age-related palsy, she twitched aside the blanket covering her legs. "I'll need your assistance in a moment."

Esme moved forward, expecting Miriam was about to get up. But that wasn't what happened at all. Instead, Miriam vanished.

In the chair, nestled in shawls and blankets, there was no longer an elderly human woman, but a very, very old fox. Her muzzle was white with age, but her rheumy eyes were still sharp. She looked up at Esme's astonished face and seemed to grin. An instant later, she was human again.

Esme helped her back into her clothes. "Well ... that is a surprise. I never guessed, not even once."

"You're surprised, but not shocked," Miriam said. "I thought so." She leaned close, and whispered, "And what are you, dear?"

Esme hesitated for only the briefest moment. "A dragon."

Miriam's eyes widened briefly. "A dragon. Goodness. I've heard of your kind, but I wasn't sure if you were real or not ..." She winked. "At least until I saw your boyfriend shift."

"Oh, *Heikon*," Esme sighed. "He's so sure that humans don't pay attention to what's going on around them. He's not half as careful as he should be. When did you see him?"

"Months ago now, dear. One of the times Sarah was driving me to class early. I just happened to be looking out the window in the right direction to see a dark shadow descend through the rain, and a moment later your beau was stepping out from behind a building, shaking rain off his umbrella." She smiled. "You dragon shifters really do keep your clothes when you shift. That's convenient."

"Convenient in some ways, but I doubt if Heikon would be so cavalier about shifting if he had to walk around naked afterwards." Though ... the idea was rather nice. Hmmm.

"I can't believe I've met not just one dragon, but two," Miriam mused. "I don't suppose you'd mind if I told Sarah? I'll keep it a secret if you want me to."

"Your granddaughter is also a shifter?" Esme asked. Miriam nodded. "Well ... I guess that'd be okay. I don't want it spread around, though."

Miriam touched her finger to the side of her nose. "Urban foxes are sly. And good at keeping secrets."

Indeed they were. Esme thought for a moment of inviting Miriam to the wedding, but it was much too far for such an old woman to travel, even an old fox. "I appreciate you trusting me enough to tell me," she said instead.

Miriam held out her hand, and Esme clasped the cold, trembling fingers in her own. "And you as well," the old woman said quietly.

After that, it was conversation and cake and, of course, dancing. The party lingered through the evening, until finally everyone began to collect their coats and say good night.

"Wait," Esme called. "Thank you, all of you. Before you go, I wanted to give you something."

She passed around keys, each one folded in a slip of paper.

"This is a key to the front door, and the security code. I'm going to be gone for a while, and I don't know when I'll be back. If you want to come in whenever I'm gone and use the ballroom, please feel free. My apartment will be locked, but I'll leave some records and CDs downstairs for you."

"But you will be back?" Judy asked, folding her hand over the piece of paper, and it was clear from the looks on all of their faces that she was speaking for the entire group.

"Yes," Esme said, smiling.

She and Heikon were still working out the details, but it was looking like they'd probably spend half the year at the mountain, and the other half in the city. Esme was already thinking it might be nice to have a summer getaway, and then all winter long for working on her music and teaching her students, with restaurants and symphonies and nice stores to shop in.

The future was looking bright. Brighter than it ever had.

"Yes," she said again, more firmly. "I'll be back."

EPILOGUE

There were few things to compare with the wedding of a dragon clanlord, with the entire clan in attendance.

The clan had been busy for weeks, hunting game for a tremendous feast and decorating the entire mountain with flowers. And then the guests began to arrive. Heikon had been clanlord for a very long time, and he'd accumulated a lot of friends and allies among the other clans. There were representatives from nearly every one of the major clans, as well as most of Esme's clan, the red-haired, aristocratic Lavignas mingling somewhat awkwardly with Heikon's more down-to-earth, rural clan.

Heikon's mother was there, joining them for a clan function for the first time in a very long time.

Darius Keegan was there, with his visibly pregnant mate Loretta. Ben and Tessa were there, Darius's son with the former keeper of the Heart of Heikon's hoard—now retired to a simple life as a wife and mother and (from what Heikon had heard) the founder and leader of a cat rescue. Given what he'd seen of Tessa, he could only imagine that a great many cats were going to be rescued.

Melody and Gunnar were there, with little Dash and Daria wrapped up in blankets. It looked like neither of the twins had started to shift yet. With one dragon parent and one bear parent, there was no telling what kind of shifters they were going to turn out to be. But Heikon could tell—watching Esme bending over her grandchildren, and seeing the joy on Melody's face to match her mother's—that no matter what the children shifted into, they would be loved.

He and Esme had a simple ceremony in the sakura grove. It was long past spring flowering time, but the young trees rose straight and green. At the end of the ceremony, each of them planted a seed, and then select members of the clan came forward and planted seeds of their own, including Reive.

Heikon found himself watching Reive carefully. The young man had never seemed to fully recover after being injured. He was still unusually pale, and moved slowly and carefully. Even now, as Reive straightened up and handed his shovel to Anjelica, Heikon saw him turn away from her and then wince involuntarily, starting to raise a hand to touch his arm before he dropped it again.

"One moment, my love," Heikon murmured, and left Esme to talk to her clanmates, weaving among the crowd to join Reive.

As soon as he saw his uncle, Reive smoothed out his face, the look of pain vanishing.

"Are you all right, nephew?"

"I'm fine," Reive said. He smiled. "Just a twinge from an old wound; it's nothing. I don't know about you, but I'm ready for the buffet table. I've been smelling that meat cooking all morning."

Heikon meant to follow up on it, but Reive was moving

fine now, as if the moment of weakness had only been an aberration. After all, there was no telling how long it took to recover from gargoyle poison; such a thing was unknown before. Heikon himself had taken years to fully recover from the dragonsbane—twenty years, in fact, if the loss of the mate bond counted as a wound.

Esme slipped into his personal space, slim and graceful. She had opted not to wear a traditional wedding dress; instead she was dressed in green and white, with a crown of flowers in her long, unbound hair. She was, as always, gorgeous enough to put his gardens to shame.

"My mate," he murmured, taking her hand and bringing it to his lips. "My wife."

Esme beamed at him, and all other thoughts were washed away in the sunlight-on-leaves gleam of her green eyes. The bond between them thrummed gently with her pleasure and joy.

"I think this day is perfect except for one thing," she said, and raised a hand.

From somewhere among the trees, music began to play. Heikon had seen them out here earlier, Esme directing a dozen younger members of the clan as they strung wire around the gardens and set up stereo equipment. Now the garden filled with music, and his heart filled with love.

"My love," Esme murmured. "Shall we dance?"

Heikon closed his eyes and leaned into her arms, and there was nothing in the world but contentment and joy for him, for *them*, and the promise of a future far beyond his wildest dreams.

I t was not to the buffet that Reive went, but instead deep into the gardens. The bowers of roses, the dense stands of flowers and foliage closed around him, shutting out the world.

If there was one thing Uncle's gardens were good at, it was providing private places to hide. He'd known that since he was a kid.

He sank onto a stone bench under one of the bowers. Roses growing on a wooden trellis shielded him from view, but he would hear anyone coming by the crunching of their feet on the gravel path. Anyway, as the music began out of sight, he figured everyone would be too busy to bother him for a while.

His right arm ached down to the bone. It was the kind of pain that comes from severe cold, the sort of pain when your hands are so chilled that even the bones hurt. Like an ice-cream headache but deep in the body.

It was sometimes better, sometimes worse, and sometimes, like today, it distracted him so he could hardly think. But ever since his poisoning, he hadn't been free of it.

And now there was something else. Wincing, he rolled up his sleeve.

The gargoyle's poison spikes had left a row of small, puckered scars on his arm. This was unusual; shifters did not normally scar. But it wasn't unheard-of. A bad enough wound could still leave scars behind.

And at first, scars were all they had been.

Now each of them had become grayish and hard, numb to the touch. Each patch of grayish skin was about the size of a dime. They marched up his arm where the spikes had struck him, almost up to his shoulder.

Reive was pretty sure they hadn't been quite that big yesterday.

He prodded at one of them. It was cold and hard to the touch. When he tapped it, his fingernail clicked against stone.

His right hand lay in his lap. He turned it over and flexed it. To all outward appearances, it looked normal, and he couldn't tell if it was just his imagination that it seemed to respond more sluggishly than it used to. He flexed his hand a few more times, and felt a sharp twinge of pain race up his arm.

He turned his arm so he could look at it again. Two of the dime-size spots of stone, the two that were closest together, now had a thread of stone connecting them. He prodded at it, and found it hard to the touch, like something embedded under the skin. The flesh ached around it.

Reive let out a shuddering breath and slumped against the back of the bench. He rolled down his sleeve before anyone could see.

What he had feared was true. He was turning to stone.

~

Continue reading Reive's story in STONESKIN DRAGON, available now!

A NOTE FROM ZOE CHANT

Thank you for buying my book! I hope you enjoyed it. If you'd like to be emailed when I release my next book, please click here to be added to my mailing list: http://www. zoechant.com/join-my-mailing-list/. You can also visit my webpage at zoechant.com or follow me on Facebook or Twitter. You are also invited to join my VIP Readers Group on Facebook!

Please consider reviewing *Dancer Dragon*, even if you only write a line or two. I appreciate all reviews, whether positive or negative.

If you're dying to know what happens to Reive, **Stoneskin Dragon**, Reive and Jess's book, is available now!

Cover art: © Depositphoto.com

~

If you enjoyed this book, you might also like my paranormal romance and sci-fi romance written as Lauren Esker!

Shifter Agents

Handcuffed to the Bear

Guard Wolf

Dragon's Luck

Tiger in the Hot Zone

Shifter Agents Boxed Set #1

(Collecting *Handcuffed to the Bear, Guard Wolf,* and *Dragon's Luck)*

Standalone Paranormal Romance

Wolf in Sheep's Clothing

Keeping Her Pride

Warriors of Galatea

Metal Wolf

Metal Dragon

Metal Pirate